Libations for the Dead

Justice/Vengeance

Volume 1

Erik Scott de Bie

Other Lady Vengeance Stories

The Justice/Vengeance Series
Libations for the Dead (2023, DefCon One Publishing)

Other Stories
"Vengeance on the Layover" originally published in the *Cobalt City Timeslip* anthology (Timid Pirate Publishing, 2010)

"Angels of Mercy," originally published in the *Triumph over Tragedy* anthology (Terrene Press, 2013)

"The Curse of the Bambino," originally published in the *This Mutant Life: Bad Company* anthology (Kalamity Press, 2013)

"Queen of Demons," originally published in the *Monster Hunter: The Good Fight* anthology (Emby Press, 2015)

"Baggage," originally published in the *Shadowed Souls* anthology (Roc, 2016)

"Mother of Harlots," originally published in the *Dragonstorm* anthology (DefConOne Publishing, 2022)

Eye for an Eye (originally published as a part of *Cobalt City Double Feature*, 2012, Timid Pirate Publishing; reprinted 2018, DefCon One Publishing)

Femmes Fatale, with Amanda Cherry (2022, DefCon One Publishing)

CONTENTS

Dedication   Pg 1

Acknowledgements   Pg 3

Kickstarter Backers   Pg 5

1. Waking Up on the Dark Side of the Bed   Pg 7

2. Adored by Millions   Pg 13

3. The Heir Unapparent   Pg 19

4. Whiskey for Remembrance   Pg 25

5. The Professor   Pg 33

6. Calling in the Muscle   Pg 39

7. Happy Hour   Pg 41

8. The Well of All Fears   Pg 49

9. Party Crashers   Pg 53

10. A Better Warrior   Pg 59

11. Scheduling   Pg 65

12 Boxing While Blonde   Pg 69

13. Love Pink   Pg 73

14. All by Myself   Pg 81

15. Guidance Counseling   Pg 83

16. Safe Harbor   Pg 87

17. Round Two   Pg 91

18. Into the Deep End   Pg 97

19. The All-Seer   Pg 105

20. What Could Go Wrong?   Pg 109

21. Nemesis: Execute   Pg 115

22. Do You Even Fight, Sis?   Pg 123

23. Grouping and Regrouping   Pg 129

24. Domestic Disaster   Pg 137

25. Past Sins   Pg 143

26. Breaking Stuff   Pg 151

27. Business as Usual   Pg 161

28. Postnasal Drip   Pg 171

29. No More Running   Pg 179

30. Shock and Awe   Pg 195

Epilogue: Flying   Pg 205

About the Author   Pg 213

For my readers. You're the best.

ACKNOWLEDGEMENTS

No story is wholly a creation of the author's mind, and this one is no exception. So many voices and ideas went into producing this novel, which is twenty years in the making. I drew concepts and images from Brian Michael Bendis, Garth Ennis, Robert Kirkman, Kelly Sue DeConnick, Gail Simone, and other comic titans. Long ago, old friends helped me develop the story, including Jacob, both the Dereks, and the rest of my gang back when I first created the concept. The Cobalt City crew, including its creator Nathan Crowder, my initial recruiter Rosemary Jones, my co-author on *Femmes Fatale* Manda Cherry, my editor Dawn Vogel, and Jeremy Zimmerman, who also doubles as the publisher at DefConOne. Also the other Agents of Awesome: Mathew, Kai, Red, Stick, Amanda, and Kels (who has also produced a lot of awesome art for my characters and stories). Special credit to one of my favorite editors to work with, Kerrie Hughes, who edited the *Shadowed Souls* anthology and pushed Lady V that extra bit.

The influence of all these fine creators ultimately made it possible for me to put this book out in the world, and impossible for me not to put it out. Thank you.

KICKSTARTER BACKERS

The following awesome individuals pledged to support this project!

Demand Vengeance!
Kelsey Dawn Scott aka Wren "The Shrike" Fulton-Gray

Supergroup!
Bryan "Quadroman" Maus, Chris Shipley, Sean Eric Fagan, The Masked Butler

Bartenders!
Lynda Shirreffs, Rynn "Masterwork" Idhril, Vi "Mini Boss" Tran

Last Call Regulars!
Austin "Rainbow Mini" Buelt, Ben "Bone Fingers" Dobyns, Carlos Ovalle, Derek Lindbloom, Dominic Franchetti, Doug "the Merchant" Meyer, Kai "The King in Red" Ford, Logan Bonner, Nancy West Johnson aka "The Digital Celt", Randy Mcfadden, Scratchpad Publishing, The Year TWO THOUSAND

Patrons!
Alexandra Pitchford, Alice in Wonderland, Amanda Ratchford Cherry aka "Ruby Killingsworth", Andrea Brandt, Brian "Loremaster" James, Bruce "Rampage" Cordell, Caroline "Seadog" Dombrowski, Chad Brown, Chris A. Jackson, Chris Tulach, Collin Shaneyfelt, Daniel Helmick, Daniel Kemler, Darren Morrissey, Derek Guder, Dwayne Farver, Eboni Obanero, Elizabeth Tereno, Eric C., Eric Slaney , Erica "Vulpinfox" Schmitt, Erick "The

Recluse" Christgau, Erin M. Evans, Gabrielle Harbowy, Gerald "The Corner of Story and Game" Ford, Gina "Catloverbooklover" Costa Jones, Insane Angel Studios, J.M. Saul, James "Do Hung" LEE, James Baker, Jimmy Campbell, Jason Hatter, Jeff Pfaff, Jil "The Goddess" Scott, Joel Everett, Josh Vogt, Katherine Monasterio, Kian "The Fox" Grey, Lori "Jadehorn" Krell, Lynne "The Empress" de Bie, Matt Youngmark, Nick "Epic Realms" Sampson, Robert N. Emerson, Sara "Kick" Johnston, Sarah Grant, Scott James Magner, SE. Grizz, Sean K. Reynolds, Spike Murphy, Stephanie Bryant, Torrey Podmajersky, Travis Armstrong, VonEther, Will "Willie G" Lorenzo, Zan Christensen

1. WAKING UP ON THE DARK SIDE OF THE BED

Some years ago, Vivienne Cain reached a point in her life where her dreams became significantly, undeniably better than her real life.

And the best ones always come in the morning, in those last panicked minutes before she has to get up. Which is, not coincidentally, part of why she usually sleeps until noon or later.

The booze is another reason.

Her phone buzzes at 9 a.m., cutting through a particularly good dream. Not *now*.

Skin caresses skin, lips and tongue trail along the hollow of her neck, and she can't help but smile and gasp. She loses herself in the feeling, riding the wave.

Again the phone buzzes. The half-dream fractures as sound and light intrude, leaving only fragmentary impressions and fleeting memories. Images and sensory data. A hand, clutching hers. A strong body pressed against her back. The smell of wilting lilies. Black thorns. Her legs wrapped tightly around—someone. Warmth. Hunger. *Need*.

Vivienne wakes up alone. Again.

"Dammit," she says, voice muffled in the tangled, sweaty sheets. The tattoo stretching down her arm looks like a whipping vine of thorns as she fumbles for the phone. The flashing blue screen guides her hand under the pillow, where it has almost fallen off the bed.

Caller unknown. What's the point of these damn things if they can't even identify a caller?

She taps the green button and discards the phone back onto the mattress. "What."

"It's me."

Of course it is. Who else would it be?

"Fuck you," she says.

Of course it doesn't work.

"It's that day," the voice says.

Of course it's that day.

"You're going, right?"

Vivienne means to say *fuck off*, but all that comes out is "mmrff."

"You're going. I can tell."

"Whatever." A churning mass of profanity rises up Vivienne's throat, or maybe it's just bourbon and whatever starchy thing she ate last night. She keeps it down with some effort. "See you there."

"Doubt it."

The call ends with three soft beeps.

Fuck.

Vivienne lies there unmoving in the rumpled tangle, fitted sheet half pulled off the same ratty mattress she's slept on for ten years. The pillow has a faint but delicious smell: sleep and an escaped dream. But as hard as she drives her face into the softness in a vain attempt to recapture sleep, that voice won't get out of her head. Her heart thuds in her throat. Her mouth feels like the desert.

The apartment intrudes as well, as it always does when her body claws toward sobriety. It feels like it always does: hazy and empty. Too modern to have acquired much in the way of the mishmash of energies that accumulate in such a place, which she likes about it. It almost feels safe.

People talk about ghosts, and this is most of what they mean. Every occupant leaves a different resonance, its strength depending mostly on the length of their stay, and Vivienne is pretty sure only a couple of people lived in her unit before her. It has since picked up her own familiar signature—mostly apathy with hints of lust and despair—which suits her just fine. Her constant state of at least mild inebriation blocks out the feelings of the other occupants of the apartment complex, and she works nights so she's usually not around to absorb their strongest passions.

Being an empath blows, almost as much as being a (mostly) functioning alcoholic.

God, she needs a drink.

She rolls over and stares up at the listlessly turning ceiling fan. It's been an unseasonably warm January for Seattle, and the spring and summer are going to be worse. It's like she's melting in her bed and not in a good way.

Her mind keeps going over a joke Andre told her yesterday, that it's a good thing all that climate change business is a hoax, or else we'd really be fucked. Something like that. Something funnier, probably. If it weren't for Andre, the world would be a pretty shitty place, all around.

Vivienne hauls herself up to a sitting position and stares down at the phone, which glows with a new text. Again the number is unknown, and the message just says: "today's the day."

"That makes me feel all better," she says to no one. "Oh wait."

A different voice speaks in her head then, and it makes her shiver into full awareness.

Today, the demon says.

Vivienne sits suddenly very still, all her muscles taut. Did—did she really hear that?

Whether it's a memory or not, she isn't about to take the chance. Her heart beats out of her chest. Her groping hands find the half-empty fifth of bourbon on the bedside table, and she makes it three-quarters empty. The liquor steadies her. Makes her heart slow. Makes the demon fall silent.

Now she's just left with today. Great.

She pulls on black panties and, using the walls to keep upright, wanders to the bathroom to pee. Her toilet is on the opposite side of the tiny bathroom from the sink, so she has to confront herself whether she likes it or not, and she never does. Shit. The mirror's always a cock, but today it's particularly dickish: dark circles under her eyes, redness around her nose, skin could be better. Her hair looks like two panthers tried to kill each other. Probably should take a shower, but fuck it.

Back in the bedroom, as a train zooms past her open window, she gets dressed the rest of the way: her least awful black bra, black jeans faded to gray, and the first shirt she can grab from her dresser. It's black with the words "Nasty Woman" in plain white letters across the front. It's either that or the one with the peeling logo of the cute little goth girl in purple and white. She's not sure where she got that shirt, but she's had it forever. It can stay in the drawer at least another day.

She looks up at the window and finds herself face to face with a number of staring faces pressed to the windows of the train raised to the level of her second-floor apartment. Occasionally, the monorail stops right outside her window, but that isn't a compelling enough reason to shut the drapes, particularly when it's so warm. They stare at one another—the passengers and the forty-something woman with the tattoos and mussed hair—until the train shudders into motion.

Figures. Vivienne pulls her shirt on.

She goes to shut the drawer, but something silver underneath the goth girl shirt catches her eye. Slowly, Vivienne reaches in and touches the cool metal of the hand harness, its bladed fingers coiled in on themselves like the legs of a huge, dead spider. She pulls it out, careful not to cut herself, and slides her fingers into the glove. The talons—twice the length of her fingers—click metallically against one another, glittering in the glare through the window. She wore a number of different claws as Lady Vengeance, and this is her last: a titanium alloy reinforced with RCC fibers, extremely durable and very light, perfect for cutting through anything.

Even me, says a voice from behind her.

Vivienne whirls, fingers clawed and threatening without a conscious thought, but there's no one there. She stands alone in her messy bedroom—pillows strewn haphazardly, dresser drawers open to different lengths, the floor covered with laundry. Dimly, she hears sirens in the distance, but otherwise everything seems normal. She's alone.

Even if she doesn't *feel* alone and never has.

Not even when she was a child, before the demon.

"Fuck you," she says.

The room doesn't respond, the way it usually doesn't.

Vivienne strips off the glove with a fumbling effort and throws it on the bed. The blades sink into the bare mattress with as little effort as it would take to plunge them into flesh. *Fuck.*

Vivienne shrugs into her black leather jacket—black on black—and grabs the mostly empty bourbon as a matter of course. This she stuffs into the mostly empty black purse Andre makes her carry around to look normal. Sigh.

She reaches for her bike helmet and remembers only belatedly that she took the bus home yesterday, and her motorcycle's still at the bar. Andre hooked her up with an Orca pass and slipped the card into her jacket pocket.

She gives him crap about taking care of her, but it reassures her.

The claw is sitting on the bed, two of the fingers poking into the mattress. Yellow fluff peeks out around the blades. Add it to the damage.

Why the fuck not.

Vivienne grabs the claw and stuffs it in her purse.

She slams the door on her way out.

2. ADORED BY MILLIONS

Just northwest of downtown, Belltown has historically contained a lot of what makes Seattle the city it is. The Space Needle, for one, with the carnival and skeeball machines at its feet, and the Museum of Popular Culture just a stroll away, with the Science Center and its massive movie screen in the opposite direction. All of them are located in Seattle Center, with its little mall and candy stores, surrounded by theaters and performance halls like a cultural beacon for the Pacific Northwest. Great bars and trendy shops, all walkable. Also, Vivienne's favorite peeping tom: the monorail that all Seattle residents either loved or hated passionately ten years ago and have now largely forgotten exists. The city's still in the process of removing the Viaduct just south of the neighborhood, and a lot of tourists ride the monorail these days. There's a thriving drug market, too, and gentrification has done only a little to diminish the crack deals happening in broad daylight.

In short, it's the perfect place to hide, as Vivienne Cain has been doing for a decade.

No sooner does she step out onto the street from the Bellhooks Apartments driveway than she hears the sirens she noticed earlier screaming in the near distance, as well as car horns going crazy down Fourth Avenue. Cracks of gunfire fill the air not too far away. A bright red car careens madly through the morning traffic, and bullets fly from one of the passengers back at the pursuing cop cars.

The people on the street, not accustomed to these kinds of sights, react in predictable ways. Some scramble away, falling over themselves to escape the oncoming chaos. Some stare mutely, their brains unable to process what's happening. Some start calling 911, as if the police aren't already on it. Some start screaming. Some start recording it with their phones. Vivienne knows all this without looking, because she can taste their rising fear and, beneath that, the sharp sweetness of wonder.

Not enough booze this morning to block out that much emotion, it seems.

Thanks to decades of training and experience, Vivienne doesn't react in any of these ways, but instead assesses the situation like the experienced fighter she is. Late model Japanese getaway car— Honda Accord, she thinks. Probably a fortunate carjacking: fortunate, because Accords have enough pickup to compete in straight races, and a carjacking because no self-respecting criminal drives a red sedan to a robbery. Her sharp eyes pick up four men, probably all armed, the driver halfway skilled. She can think of half a dozen ways to intervene, a couple that would even minimize loss of life.

It doesn't matter, though, because of the pink streak she sees in the sky down the street, just past a massive billboard. It roars through the air toward her, after the racing Accord with the robbers. Vivienne steps back into the shade of the complex's arched entrance. She knows what's about to happen. A couple of people are standing stupidly in front of the fire station across the street, and Vivienne shoots them a sharp glance, backed with a little fear energy. The jolt shocks them out of stupor and into flight mode, and they scramble away.

There. Her good deed for the day.

Roughly parallel with the fire station, the robbers are close enough for Vivienne to hear them shouting and taste their rage and growing panic. One of them sees the pink streak hurtling toward them like a comet, and Vivienne gets a shot of confused terror. He's fumbling with a weapon.

Vivienne sees the shape of a young woman among the flames, one arm stretched forward.

Then she slams into the side of the Accord, like a defender tackling a running back out of bounds, and the car goes flying out of the street. It spins in a corkscrew maneuver and smashes through one of the big red doors, right into a fire engine whose engine just started up. The vehicles crunch each other to a halt with a mournful mewling of the truck's horn. The Accord ends up upside down, halfway outside the fire station, its wheels spinning crazily.

Big dudes in dark blue outfits with neon green stripes go running, and Vivienne has a moment's regret for the poor muscular firemen. Not only has the accident blocked them from getting out on a call, but now they have all this to deal with. Bad day. Maybe if she could stick around, comfort one of them—or two, or three— but obviously this isn't a safe place for her to stay.

She should just get on the bus and leave, but part of her has to see this.

The exposed door of the Accord shudders twice, then swings open with a disconsolate sigh. One of the criminals comes crawling out, his face covered in blood, and lies gasping on the sidewalk. His weapon—a Tec-9 missing its magazine—clatters out ahead of him, out of his clumsy fingers. As a shadow descends onto him, he reaches out one shaking hand to pick it back up.

"Ah ah," says a woman's voice.

A tall white boot descends onto his wrist, nailing him to the ground like a hammer, and the man utters a mewling cry. Vivienne feels the spike of revulsion as his bones break, which the woman in the pink flames probably didn't intend, but if the car going into the fire station proves nothing else, it's that she doesn't know her own strength. Amateur.

"Stay down, ok? Ok."

She stands over the captured robber, one hand on her hip in a model-esque pose, sleek in her white body suit with pink piping and about half covered with various corporate logos. Her suit splits the difference between an Olympic athlete's warm-up tracksuit and a NASCAR uniform, up to and including an aerodynamic white helmet with the pink letter "A" over the visor. A dozen phones record her appearance, and voices clamor around her. Give the inexperienced hero one thing, it's a talent for an opportunistic photo op.

"All right, all right, hang on," she says. "Geez, you guys are fast."

The woman reaches up to pull her helmet off, revealing a tumbling mass of bleached gold hair, brown skin drawn tight around her perky cheekbones, and sparkling silver eyes. She's young—maybe seventeen or eighteen—but she looks well accustomed to all the attention and accolades. She gives them her trademark cocky smile, and that earns her about a hundred thousand hits on social media.

In the background, the same teenager, wearing a white and pink bikini, is on the big pink billboard advertising a perfume called "Innocence."

That's A-Girl for you.

Vivienne clicks her tongue.

And the world in general.

~

"A-Girl!" People shout her name. "A-Girl!"

So many flashes go off in her face that Angel DeSantes is dazzled without the helmet. Maybe taking it off was a mistake. Too late now. She smiles brilliantly and tries not to flinch.

She's A-Girl: celebrity superhero, daughter of legends. Half-Latina, half-goddess. She has a crimefighting career to think of. And an acting career. And a music one. (She's a triple threat.)

"That was amazing, A-Girl!" someone says, and another voice says, "I love you, A-Girl!"

"Love you back," she says to a chorus of squeals.

Reporters are on the scene in under a minute, and the cops are more than happy to let them at her while they deal with the crime scene. Posters and notepads extend her direction for signatures, and she pulls out one of the dozen pink pens she carries around for just this purpose. Before Angel can remember one of the catchphrases her agent drilled her on, she's got a dozen reporters around her, extending microphones in her way, and her mind mostly goes blank.

"A-Girl!" a man asks. "Nathan Crown, KUOW. How did you get on the scene so fast?"

"Oh, you know, I was in the neighborhood," Angel says. "Just, like, flying around?"

"On patrol?" Crown asks, taking notes on his tablet.

"Right," she says. Then, with a smile: "I'm fast. Like, *really* fast."

That earns some applause. More voices clamoring for her attention. "A-Girl! A-Girl!"

So far, so ok.

"A-Girl, Christine Foley, Q13 FOX. What can you tell us about your new video?" a woman asks. "When does it drop? And will it be as much of a hit as 'Just A-Girl'?"

"Any day now, and I hope so," she says. "But what do I know? I'm just A-Girl."

Ugh, that sounded really tired, but Parker insisted. Her agent is so corny.

"A-Girl—A-Girl!" a man calls. "When do you turn eighteen?"

"Ew," Angel says, forcing herself to smile wider. Like that was flattering and not just creepy.

Smile and nod, she thinks.

"What's the 'A' stand for?" someone asks, as they always do.

A-Girl takes a steadying breath. "Oh, I dunno—" she says, as she always does.

"A for Awesome!" someone in the crowd shouts, even as someone else shouts "A for Amazing!" Then there's "A for A Plus Plus!" and then some hipster says, "A for Aardvark," and everyone laughs. It's a typical sound bite.

Remember who you are. *What* you are. You chose this, didn't you?

Sometimes, she wonders.

"A-Girl! A-Girl!"

There are more questions—more flashing lights—but she isn't in the moment anymore. Instead, Angel looks across the street, where the sidewalk has mostly cleared out. Most of the passersby either rushed her immediately or snuck a few glances and then went on their way. One woman, however, stands and stares at her. She's forty-ish and dark, and not just because of her black-on-black clothes or her raven hair. The darkness sticks to her, as if the sunlight dims around her. Like a permanent, invisible umbrella. Her eyes are the color of a rich Pinot Noir, sweet on the nose but sure to make you choke. And the intensity of her stare grabs Angel's attention and won't let go, like her eyes are hands grabbing her first by the shoulders, then working their way to her neck.

Just like that, the moment ends, and at first Angel isn't sure where the woman went.

She wonders, for a moment, if—

But no, that's not possible. Vivienne Cain has been dead for years, since Angel was just a kid. She died the day she ruined

17

Angel's idyllic little life, tearing out her dad's eye and getting her mom killed. There was no way she survived that day.

Right?

Suddenly, the cameras make her ill, and she can't smile any more. "Sorry, I—I have to go."

Angel bends her legs slightly, collecting energy in swirling pink ribbons. Then she explodes up from the pavement into the sky like a rocket, making all the photographers, reporters, and fans stagger back. Some cry out in pain from the sudden heat, while many keep clamoring questions.

She flies away into the Seattle morning.

3. THE HEIR UNAPPARENT

"From dust was I born, and to dust I will return," the priest says. "In faith do I live, and in that faith I place my trust—"

Wind sweeps through Calvary, sending a flurry of brown and red leaves swirling among the graves and drowning out the rest of the prayer. Which is fine, because Marcus Orestes isn't listening.

Some of the deceased's friends from the nursing home are watching him close. Judging. It makes some part of him uncomfortable. He's not sure what to say or how he's supposed to feel, standing there and holding his coat closed tight against the wind. So he just looks down at his mother's coffin as they lower it into the grave.

"For the law of the spirit of life has made me free from the law of sin and death."

Her favorite verse. Unusual, but Marcus never got a chance to learn much about her. Maybe if he had, it would make sense.

"For those who live according to the flesh set their minds on the things of the flesh—"

He met Anita Houston just last week, after his roommate found a letter amongst his pile of unaddressed mail. Chuck gets delivery after delivery every day: bills, Amazon deliveries, credit card offers, ask letters from charities, Kickstarter rewards, packs full of coupons, junk mail of all kinds. He refuses to put his name on any lists, which includes no-mail lists, and prides himself on going through all the resulting clutter eventually. Marcus, by contrast, never gets any mail: his dads have embraced email, and he's careful not to sign any petitions. Plus he spent the last month studying for midterms, so he wasn't watching the mail.

Thus, the letter from Marcus's mother waited for a week or two, hidden between an appeal from Mercy Corps and an unmarked envelope containing a credit card application.

"Dear Marcus," it said. "You don't know me, and that's my fault. I'm sorry."

He remembers Chuck watching him while he read it. His hands trembled on the paper.

"I'm your mother, and I have to see you."

There was more, but that's what he remembers. And an address.

Marcus met with her. Of course he did. She was forty, maybe, but what patches of kinky hair remained had gone mostly white and brittle like old cobwebs. Her brown hand seemed so much lighter than his own, withered with the tag-team of cancer and chemo. She felt thin—like a mostly emptied box of envelopes forgotten in the back room. Her bones were dried out twigs wrapped in skin like paper.

Ms. Houston. *Anita*. It was hard to think of her as his mother.

"I've ... made so many mistakes," she said. "I never should ... never should have given you up."

"It's—it's ok," he said, which was all he could manage, but it sounded pathetic. Even now, four days later, he can't say if he was angry or sad or what.

"But those who live according to the spirit, the things of the spirit—"

The memory mingles with the priest's speech. Anita Houston looks like an angel in his memory, illumined in the thin light from the window. A withered angel, with all the goodness and light in her squeezed out and evaporated. The priest assures him that the Lord shall walk beside her for all the days to come. But there won't be any more days. She was out of time even when he met her.

He can't help but wonder what he would have done if he'd found the letter a week earlier, when his mother first sent it. Maybe it's for the best he didn't. He could barely speak to her as it was—if they'd had more time, maybe it would have been worse.

"I need to tell you," she said, "about your father."

Marcus catches his breath.

His father.

"For thou art with me, I shall fear no evil," says the priest.

He never knew his birth parents. David Orestes and Sean Joyce adopted him when he was less than a year old. He went through a period of time in his teens where the idea of biological parents kept him up at night, and he fought with his dads about it a few times. But sometime between graduating high school and his first year at UW, he pretty much let go of the idea. Now that birth parents were suddenly a real thing, he didn't know what to think.

"We were never married, you know," she said. "He rescued me, and—well, I knew I shouldn't. So did he. But he—" She coughed, and the nurse brought her a glass of water. It took a minute for her to catch her breath again. "He needed me, and I needed him. I won't apologize for it, you hear?"

"Yes, ma'am." Marcus nodded, not a doubt in his mind.

She had an authoritative way about her. Ms. Houston had been a schoolteacher, they said, down in Rainier Beach. Far removed from his own comfortable life up in Magnolia, where his dads provided the best schools and all the internet he could want. They were so wealthy, and she so poor.

He still hasn't told his dads about Ms. Houston, and he isn't sure he will.

If he'd known about her earlier, could he have made her life better? Would they have caught the cancer earlier, and maybe saved her? So she wouldn't end up like this—a dried up skeleton in a box?

Ms. Houston leaned back in the bed, and her glazed eyes sparkled just a little. "I loved him," she said. "I need you to know that. That's where you come from. Your people. You need to know."

Marcus nodded again. "Who," he asked. "Who was he?"

She was mostly gone, then. Rasping. Shivering. Nurses hovered anxiously outside her door. The DNR gave them some privacy, and it was almost over.

"Your father—" She coughed as she said the name, and at first Marcus thought she'd said, "just us." Then she cleared her throat and said it again, louder and with pride.

"Your father ... was Justice."

Marcus was confused. Maybe the cancer wasn't just in her lungs and ovaries but in her brain.

She gestured to the side table—would have picked up the folded-up newspaper if she could. He picked it up for her and started to hand it to her, but she pointed to the picture on the front page below the fold. The newspaper was slightly yellow with age, but he could make out the picture of the most famous team of heroes in the world: Supergroup.

They were pictured at an awards ceremony fifteen years ago, when he would have been just a kid. Glowing goddess Athena, with her burnished armor and spear, looking serene and beautiful as ever. Dark, brooding, tech-armored vigilante The Raven, who still had both eyes. Wise-cracking Kid Aphid, who stuck to walls and spat acid, grinning like an idiot. Black sheep anti-hero Lady Vengeance, with her hair dyed red and a sour expression spoiling the mood.

And there was their leader, Justice: towering, muscular, epic Justice with his dark skin and shy smile. Justice—champion of heroes, legend among legends—who stood for truth, justice, and humanity. Defender of all things good and noble in the world.

His father.

Justice.

He's read all their comics. He knows everything about them.

But, of course, it's way too late.

About fifteen years ago—shortly after the picture was taken—a combined army of Supergroup's rogues gallery ambushed their base of operations in Seattle Center and brutally murdered the team, past and present. Almost all of them. The heroes took down most of the villains, sure, but at the cost of their own lives.

It was a bloodbath, according to the news. Athena was the first to go, spitted on more than twenty spears ripped from the walls and ceiling by some telekinetic villain whose name Marcus doesn't remember. Kid Aphid dissolved screaming in his own acidic spit. Raptorman and Sevenfist apparently killed each other, having been controlled by Mind-O-Matter, though some say the Sevenfist escaped and became a PTSD-ridden serial killer thereafter. And Lady Vengeance, well, supposedly she turned on Supergroup and fought The Raven to a standstill, tearing out one of his eyes in the process.

Of Supergroup, only three survived: the technosavant Big Head, who had by that point left the team over some disagreement to work for the U.S. government; Silver Sakura, who was paralyzed in the battle; and The Raven, who staggered out of the carnage, bleeding profusely and missing one eye. He gruffly told the first reporter he saw that Lady Vengeance had betrayed the team, that he killed her, and then he left Seattle, never looking back. Apparently, he annexed the former state of Colorado from the United States and now rules a technocracy.

And Justice?

Witnesses reported seeing Justice evaporate in a crackling red energy beam—a last, dying shot from one of his many nemeses, Blastorta. His death sent America into weeks of sadness, with more outpouring of grief than the last presidential death or national tragedy. Congress declared a day of mourning, which, while it wasn't a work holiday, was still celebrated. Thousands still gathered in Seattle every year to hold a march and a candlelight vigil.

They built a statue for him. Well, for all of Supergroup, but mostly for him. Marcus has even seen it twice—once on a class trip, and once when Sean designed the costumes for a performance of *Die Valkur* at the Seattle Opera. The memorial is a pilgrimage point for all Americans, especially those who've grown up on Supergroup's comics, as Marcus has.

And now, Justice is supposed to be his *father*? One of the greatest American heroes of the modern age? How could he, just some kid, possibly be the son of Justice?

"Mr. Houston?" someone asks, and Marcus realizes everyone is staring at him.

They mean him. He is the deceased's only family. No parents. No siblings. No one but him.

"Do you have anything you want to say, Mr. Houston?" the priest asks.

"Orestes," he says, his voice too soft for anyone to hear. Considering the circumstances, denying his birth mother seems cruel. He shakes his head. "Nah. No thanks."

They're waiting for him to do something, so he steps forward and touches the coffin briefly. The wood is cold and smooth. It feels more like plastic, and he wonders if it's real. Apparently, money for the burial and funeral came from a private donor. His mother had nothing, in the end, except the truth.

And he knows it's true, even if he has nothing to show for it.

Justice is his father.

The chords of "Amazing Grace" float through the graveyard as they lower the coffin into the ground. The funeral ends, and the few mourners gathered file out. They express their condolences to him in hushed tones, promising to check in on him—to keep in touch. He knows he won't see any of them ever again. It's the new semester. Classes to attend. A life to live.

But it's a different life now.

How is he supposed to go back to the old one?

4. WHISKEY FOR REMEMBRANCE

After a while, Marcus realizes everyone's gone, and he's standing alone by his mother's grave. Two burly guys in work shirts are hanging out by the winding path among the headstones: a black guy with his hands in his pockets and a Latino dude on a smart phone. Considering the shovels, they're waiting to fill in the grave. They nod to Marcus, and he nods back. Apparently they've worked at Calvary enough to know to give people as long as they need.

Marcus doesn't need any longer. "Thanks, man," he says.

"Peace, brother," the guy says, and they go to work.

Marcus pulls out his phone to check what time it is and makes a little frustrated noise when the screen lock flickers and hesitates to open. For some reason, he's never been good with technology. For the last year or so, every time he gets up from a chair, particularly in the computer lab on campus, without fail he gets a static electricity shock. Maybe it's the weather.

Shivering in the January chill, Marcus wanders toward the east exit from the graveyard, past the administration building. He'll walk down the hill toward Met Market and the fire station, where he can snag the 67 back to the University. With luck, he'll make his afternoon political theory class. It's a tough class, and he's got to study hard. He did pretty well in the fall, but if he wants to keep that scholarship, he needs to ...

Wait.

Marcus stops. There, fifty feet away, stands a woman all in black. At first, she looks like a crow perched on one of the headstones, but then she moves and he sees the pallor of her skin against her wild tangle of hair. He's seen disheveled homeless people up on the Ave or downtown, but this woman doesn't look like that. She needs a shower and a hairbrush, sure, but her eyes are alert and sharp.

It reminds him of something. He thinks, bizarrely, of a comic book he's read. Of a woman dressed all in black in a graveyard. Of course, she was in a costume at the time and aliens were invading, but this weirdo is unintentionally acting out the same scene, almost to the panel.

Marcus isn't sure when he started moving toward her, but now he's close enough to observe her standing over a grave marked with a stone cross. She alternates swigs from the bottle of Jack Daniels in her hand with pouring out whiskey into the frozen grass. If she's here to mourn someone, she really doesn't show it. Kinda like how he didn't, when they were burying the mother he never knew.

"Guess being a good Catholic girl finally paid off, huh." Her voice is harsh. "Cold-hearted bitch."

She could just be talking to herself, but her attention fixes on one grave in particular. Talking to a dead person, he realizes. He's intruding, and it makes him feel vaguely gross.

Then he sees something that makes him stand up straight.

The wind pulls the woman's coat back, and her left hand emerges, wrapped in leather and metal. Claws extend from her fingers, like something out of a horror movie. Straight out of a comic book. Or a newspaper—the picture his birth mother showed him.

The black hair. The dark clothes. The voice. The claw.

It is.

It's Lady Vengeance.

But that's not possible. She must be dead, right? There are theories in the fan community that she faked her death and escaped when Supergroup perished, but he's never bought into that. Not really. Ok, maybe a small part of him—the part that never really outgrew gawking at her in the comics. But to see her here—now—it's just ... He can't believe it.

"Shit," he says under his breath. What's he supposed to do?

The woman doesn't seem to see him. She pours more of the alcohol on the ground—reverently, as though it's some kind of ritual.

"I like this, you know," she says. "Having a drink with you. Now that you're dead, I don't have to listen to your crap. It's nice."

She even *talks* like Lady Vengeance. That legendary dark wit and crass, gallows humor.

Maybe it's just a cosplayer. That would make sense. A little weird, cosplaying all alone in a graveyard in the middle of the day, and talking to a corpse, but it's possible. Right?

He should just leave her alone. Should just—

Your father ... was Justice.

"Hey." He hardly trusts his voice. He sounds like the kid he is. "Excuse me, ma'am? I don't mean to bother you, but—"

Abruptly, the woman rises to her full height, straightens her coat, and starts walking the other way. She doesn't seem to have heard him, or maybe she did hear and thinks he's a creep. And he kind of is, but this is important. Who else but a member of Supergroup can answer his questions?

She's walking away, but not too fast, and his legs are longer than hers. Weaving between gravestones, he heads her off halfway to the exit and reaches out to grab her arm. "Excuse—"

She glares back over her shoulder, her eyes burning with what looks like purple fire. He recognizes her power manifestation from the comics, but at the same time realizes that no artist has ever done it justice. They always make it look like a ribbon or rays of sunlight or, at best, like something out of a video game. The truth isn't anything like that.

When the power comes boiling out of Lady Vengeance, it's like a living thing: a scream that rises like a half-forgotten nightmare. It blossoms in her eyes and surrounds Marcus, making him stagger back.

Suddenly, Lady Vengeance has disappeared, and the graveyard seems deserted. And *darker*, somehow. The sun is still high in the sky, but it might as well be overcast. He has no shadow, and the world seems to move slower than it should. Things don't fit together very well. Marcus doesn't drink all that often, and rarely to excess, but this is what he imagines it's like to be profoundly drunk.

"What the f—?"

Then Marcus realizes he's not alone. No such luck.

The earth trembles, and he ends up on his butt. The grass is cold and wet—icy, even. The sky has gone pitch black, as though

27

he just lost eight hours and the sun has gone down. Everything looks old around him: the stone corroded and crumbling, the flowers all wilted, and the vines brown and decaying. Over the rust-encrusted metal fences of the graveyard, Marcus sees the nearby buildings have become gutted, burned-out husks rather than a place someone might do business.

"Mar-cus—"

Something clutches at his feet, and he realizes it's a grasping human hand.

It surfaces as he stumbles away, pulling itself from the disturbed earth like a diver through thick, murky water. The dirt falls away from the thing's head, and Marcus sees the sheen of a dull golden tiara. It's that and the tattered robe that give her away: Athena, Golden Goddess of Supergroup, restored to something like life through Lady Vengeance's power. Her body is a grotesque, rotted corpse, with part of her neck and significant holes in her torso missing. She's been in an awful fight. Her deeply tanned skin stretches like old, dry paper over uneven bones, and brackish blood and pus flow from her nose and mouth. She opens her eyes, and they burn bright like purple-red coals in a firepit. Her cracked lips part, revealing teeth like cigarette butts and dribbling maggots down her chin.

"*Unworthy*," she says.

As he watches, Zombie-Athena wrenches a scuffed spear from the ground—a weapon that must have been brilliant and beautiful once but has become corrupt, just as she has.

"What the shit?" he asks no one. The fear makes his hands shake. He can feel his heart thudding in his throat, and he has to fight to breathe.

Marcus crabwalks back and bumps into something else that gives way under his weight. Withered brown hands fall on his shoulders, reaching for his neck, and he scrambles away. This zombie looks less familiar, but he recognizes her all the same: his *mother*. Her body is little more than a skeleton, her head all but hairless from cancer treatments, and her eyes have the same purplish glow. She screams at him, and her breath smells like spoiled eggs nestled in a compost heap.

"The flesh!" Ms. Houston says with a mad cackle. "The flesh!"

"Oh shit," Marcus is saying, without meaning to. "Oh shit. Oh shit."

Heart beating out of his chest, Marcus manages to find his feet and backs away from the two zombie women, who funnel him back toward the road through the graveyard. He wants to run, but he knows the second he turns his back, they'll grab him. He can hardly think. Athena stands imperiously, her gaze offering divine judgment. His mother just looks like she wants to eat him.

Someone is standing behind him. Something glacially cold presses against this back, sucking the heat out of him. His whole body goes taut, the muscles refusing to work, and he stands there like one of the angel statues in the graveyard. The back of his neck itches as though spiders are tickling their way down his spine.

Freezing hands wrapped in white-dyed leather spattered with blood and mud slip past his sides, under his armpits, and the fingers lace around his chest and stomach. The white gloves are scuffed and flaps of leather reveal withered brown flesh beneath. It's those gloves that identify her, as well as the straw-thin blonde hair that brushes his cheek as she leans in to whisper in his ear.

"A for *Awful*," A-Girl says.

Marcus staggers out of her grasp and looks back at her. Zombie A-Girl is less withered and decayed than the others, but her scarred, green face is clearly dead. Her white uniform with its glowing pink designs—no corporate labels—looks as though a garbage truck hit her, but it's definitely her.

"You are not worthy." Athena grows until she towers over them all. "Never worthy of *him*."

"By the spirit, you will live!" His mother clambers toward him on all fours, more like a spider than a person. Blood drips from her mouth, where sharpened teeth have chewed into her gums.

A-Girl hasn't moved, only looks distantly sad. "A for Abhorrent."

As the three close in all around him, Marcus has nowhere to go. A headstone crunches painfully against his leg, and he turns enough to slam face-first into the ground. His mother pounces on him, and her hideous weight pins him down into the cold grass.

"Not worthy of *Justice*," Athena says. "Never worthy of him."

"A for Appalling," A-Girl says, her lips turned down in a tragic frown.

"But by the flesh—" His mother leans in to bite Marcus's neck. He can feel the pressure of her yellow teeth on his skin, and they tingle like lemon juice on a cut. "By the flesh, you die."

Marcus stares at A-Girl—at her dead eyes and face. If he's going to die, at least …

~

He's still lying there in the cold grass, cringing away, chest heaving for breath. The sky is blue again, albeit half full of gray clouds. The world is once again the world.

Ok. What the hell?

They were there. He saw it. He felt it. It really happened.

He's muddy, and his face aches where he smacked it on the ground.

"It really happened," he says to himself.

The zombies are gone, and he's alone in the graveyard—except for the two gravediggers, who are staring at him from twenty feet away. "You ok, brother?" asks one of them.

That was some weird ass shit.

"Yeah." Marcus looks around, just to make sure he really is alone. "Did you—see anything?"

The guys look at each other, then over at him. "It's a little early, ain't it?" one of them asks.

"What?" Marcus rubs his aching head. Oh right. They think he's high. "It's—it's cool."

The gravediggers give him a couple weird looks, then head off. One of them murmurs something, and the other chuckles. Probably a joke about Marcus or random college students getting high in graveyards. Fair enough.

That was her. He knows it was her. But what was she doing here?

And now that the adrenaline is starting to wear off, he realizes he knows exactly what happened: that was Lady V's fear powers. The comics make it look horrific, sure, but never quite like *that*.

Marcus shakes his head to clear it, and his eyes fall on the grave Lady Vengeance was visiting. He thought at first it was a cross, and it would probably look like that to someone who didn't look closer.

But really, it's a sword stabbing into the ground. The design looks Grecian and the name ... *Athena.*

The epitaph says: *Sister. Mother. Hero.*

Shit.

Marcus spots Lady Vengeance leaning against a tree toward the northwest corner of the graveyard. She looks tired, as though she just ran ten miles. She's still wearing the claw, and its sharp talons click idly against the trunk. Then, without looking back, she sets off down the hill along 55th, heading toward the U-District.

And Marcus follows her.

5. THE PROFESSOR

Lady Vengeance walks at a brisk pace, her coat sliding behind her like a cape. She's still wearing the claw, and she doesn't seem to notice the odd looks she gets from other pedestrians. At the bottom of the hill, she crosses over into the part of Ravenna Park that cuts through Seattle like a little forested canyon and heads northwest up one of the paths. She never looks up at the trees or any of the joggers who pass. She's a woman on a mission.

And Marcus follows her.

At first, he occasionally slips behind a parked car or into an alley to avoid being spotted. It's easy to find cover once they get to the park, and if anyone notices him following her, they don't give him any weird looks. Not that he needs to have bothered being subtle. For a big-time superhero, she doesn't seem to care about being followed—and maybe she doesn't have to. The first time he tried to bother her, she smacked him down pretty hard with her fear powers, and he almost had a panic attack. Will he even make it out if she hits him again?

"Think about this," he says to himself as they head through the park. "You know who that is. What she can do." His heart thuds. "Shit, what she fucking did to me—"

She pauses, and Marcus jerks to a halt, then heads quickly up another path before she can turn around. Whether she actually looked or not, he stays on the upper path along the slope, while she follows the trail at the base of the hollow. It's a beautiful spot, but Marcus isn't calm enough to appreciate it.

"Ok," he says to himself. "Stop freaking out. Just stop."

Obviously, he continues freaking out.

33

Marcus focuses on putting one foot in front of the other. The fast hike through the cold air has made his breathing speed up, and he tries to take deep breaths. Keep quiet. Don't let her notice you.

He's following her because she knew Justice. She's probably the only person alive who can help him, though how she's alive, he has no idea. He just can't let her see him.

When they're almost out of the park, he's so wrapped up in his head that he doesn't notice her approach until she crosses his path not ten feet ahead of him. Marcus stumbles and almost falls into the mud, but he catches himself on a tree. His heart pounds like a machine gun on full auto.

Lady Vengeance glances in Marcus's direction, her eyes burning, but she's not looking at him. Rather, she's looking at one of the buildings at the other end of the big bridge that stretches over Ravenna Park. What is that, 15th Ave? Marcus doesn't know the Roosevelt neighborhood very well.

What's she looking for?

Police cars come screaming up across the bridge, and only activate their sirens when they get within fifty feet or so. It's so sudden and so startling that Marcus momentarily loses his balance. Apparently not bothered, Lady Vengeance turns away and pops the collar of her leather jacket to hide her face. She hurries on, seemingly unconcerned, and heads north along the street, wandering in an oblivious daze. The whole time, she doesn't appear to have noticed Marcus at all.

"Ok." Marcus works to calm himself down. "You're not gonna have a heart attack."

His blood is rushing way too fast in his head.

"My God," he says under his breath. "You're such an idiot."

Marcus follows her up a few more blocks, and then she makes her way into a bar and restaurant called "Devil's Due" up on 65th. Marcus crosses the street so he can scope out the place from the bus stop, so he won't look suspicious. He watches for a few minutes, but she doesn't leave the restaurant. There, he pulls his mobile out of his pocket, struggles to unlock it—he gets a little shock for his efforts just touching the thing—and taps through his contacts.

"Ok," he says. "You can do this."

The phone starts ringing.

"Come on," he says. "Pick up, pick up, pick up—"

~

About a mile away, a desk phone rings once, punctuating a faint buzz that fills the room. It smells of old books on the shelves and a tea mug that hasn't been washed out for over a month. A window overlooks the University of Washington campus, beautiful albeit a little bleak in winter. Old movie posters adorn the walls: film noir, war epics, romances, classic period pieces. One wall is given over entirely to a poster board decorated with pictures of various superheroes cut out of newspapers and magazines, especially members of Supergroup. A pair of leather sandals sits by the little couch, and a brightly colored coat hangs from the back of the door.

A scrawny, balding man sits at the desk, eyes glued to the flickering images on the computer. He's watching on his headphones, but the volume is high enough that anyone else in the room can make out the cheesy music and faint moans. He's turned his monitor away from the half-open door, at least, so the secretary outside his office can pretend not to know he's that guy who watches porn at work.

Next to his crossed bare feet up on the desk sits a nameplate that reads "Frederick Francis."

The phone rings again, and he slides the headphones down around his neck and puts his earpiece in. He clicks to answer the call. "Stand and deliver, *heh*."

The voice on the other end of the line says, "It's me, Professor."

"Orestes, hey!" Francis leans back and pats his developing gut. "I was just about to call you. I heard back from my guy at Langley about that appointment with the Head. They postponed us again."

"That's—ok, but that's not what I'm calling—"

"Look, I know it's frustrating." Francis yawns. "But when it's government we're dealing with—"

"Professor?" Someone knocks on the door.

"Just a sec, Orestes." Francis looks up with a big smile. "Michelle! What can I do for you?"

Michelle Adams is pretty, blonde, and half his age, but those are just details. She holds up a stack of stapled pages. "My report on the apologia."

"Great—hang on." He alt-tabs out of his internet browser to an Excel document. "Toss it on my desk. Good debate Friday, by the way."

"Thanks." She brightens, then points to the blue light at his ear. "Oh—you're on the phone."

"Fine, no worries," Francis says. "It's Marcus Orestes."

"Hi, Marcus!" Michelle sways her way out of the room.

"Who was that?" Orestes asks on the phone.

"Just Michelle." Francis leans back in his chair to take a good look at her retreating backside. That miniskirt and tights combination was an excellent choice, in his opinion. "I think she likes you."

"Um, ok," Orestes says on the phone. "What?"

"You don't think so?" Francis reaches for his keyboard. "*Heh.*"

"Professor, I—" Marcus pauses a beat. "I found her."

"Ok." He pulls up the video again. "Found who?"

"Her."

"Her?" Francis' finger pauses over the spacebar. "Her who?"

"Lady Vengeance."

The world slows down, and Francis sits up, drawing his hands away from the keyboard. Instead, he reaches over and pushes the door closed. "You're shitting me."

"No, I swear to God." Over the phone, Orestes sounds agitated. "I saw her in the graveyard—"

"The graveyard?" Francis's feet start drumming rapidly without his control. "Which graveyard?"

"Calvary—the one on 55th?" Orestes says. "The grave said 'Athena.' But how does that make sense? Don't you have to be Catholic to be buried in that cemetery?"

"Athena may have been a goddess, *heh*, but she was also a recovering Catholic." Francis is almost shaking now. He leans over conspiratorially. "What happened? Tell me everything."

"She—" Francis can almost hear Orestes shiver. "She did her fear thing on me."

"No shit."

"None."

Francis shudders as well, out of excitement rather than fear. He *knew* she was alive.

"I followed her," Orestes says after a pause. "I'm gonna talk to her."

"No, wait!" Francis sits up straight, heart speeding up. "Where are you?"

"Huh?" Orestes's voice sounds distant at first, like he was about to hang up. "Say again?"

"Where are you?" Francis shoves aside some papers and grabs a pen. "Specifically?"

He notes down the rough address: 65th St. NE and 12th Ave. Not far away.

"Orestes, you stay where you are," Francis says. "That woman is very dangerous. Orestes? O—?"

But the phone has gone dead. Dropped call. His desk phone shouldn't have failed like that, but maybe Orestes is in a place with bad reception. Or he hung up on him. Damn.

Francis reaches over and locks the door out of his office and pulls the shades shut. Then he pulls a sleek black mobile phone out of his pocket and pairs it to his Bluetooth. He dials.

The call goes through immediately, but at first there is only silence. Then: "Yes?"

He shivers at that silky voice—just the one word giving him chills. "It's me," he says.

"Hello, *me*."

"*Heh*, good one."

He holds up the note in one shaking hand. Devil's Due. And an address.

"You're not gonna believe this," he says. "I found her."

6. CALLING IN THE MUSCLE

"No," the man says, his words gurgling. "Please, wai—"

A fist smashes into his mouth, cutting off his pleas in a flood of spit and blood and part of a tooth. He falls mewling to the ground, groaning about his tooth. He gropes for it among the broken cement, but all he finds is a loose pebble.

"My tooth." He sounds like his tongue is too big for his mouth. "You broke my tooth…"

The bald, scarred monstrosity of a man who just punched him into the ground isn't listening. Music thunders through his Bluetooth, and he sings right along in a rich baritone, something Italian. Likely, only a music buff would recognize an acapella rendition of an aria from Gianni Schicchi. The hulking brute has never been particularly melodic as a singer, but he makes up for it in enthusiasm.

"O mio babbino caro—" He punches the man again, and blood spatters the nearby building. "—mi piace, è bello, bello."

"You—you want money? I can get you mon—"

The bruiser smashes one massive boot into the guy's midsection with a satisfying crack. Satisfying to him, anyway—not to the poor bastard he's beating. And, if he's being honest as he usually is, it could have been a better kick. The sound of creaking bones and splintered ribs hardly competes with the music in his earpiece. Better try that one more time.

He doesn't call himself the Pugilist without being the best at what he does.

"Please—" The man croaks. "Please, no—"

"Vo andare in Porta Rossa," he sings, and kicks the mark hard enough in the gut that he vomits all over the pavement. The mark

39

looks up, eyes blurry through a mess of blood and spit and stomach acid. That wild and terrified look. That's the stuff.

The Pugilist winds back for another hit—not that he needs to, but it makes the mark's eyes almost pop out in a pleasing way—and then his Bluetooth pings. The music cuts off, replaced by a very specific ringtone he programmed to only one number. "Call from," the voice says, but he turns his wind-up into clicking the button on his Bluetooth before it says the name.

He rarely speaks when just a grunt will do, but it won't do in this case. "Afternoon, boss."

"Good morning, Pug," says the voice on the other end.

"No one calls us that but you," he says, rather cheery despite his gruff southwest London accent. He holds his target up by the collar, dimly aware of the hands vaguely slapping at his forearm. "What can we do for you this fine afternoon?"

His phone beeps.

"I just sent you an address. Move immediately."

"Well," he says to the man. "Quite the lucky day, innit mate? I got business."

The guy smiles in frantic hope.

"Bit preoccupied at the moment, boss."

A hesitation on the other end. "Two minutes."

The connection clicks off. The music kicks back in.

The man whimpers. "Wha—what?"

"A comprerar l'anello!"

The Pugilist punches him square in the nose, breaking it a second time and sending blood spattering.

7. HAPPY HOUR

"Professor? Professor!" Marcus inspects the phone, which says "call failed." When he tries to dial again, it says "no service—emergency calls only."

Trying to put aside the fact that this *is* an emergency, Marcus catches his breath, then pushes through the door. The bells at the entrance jangle, and he stops on the threshold, startled.

I really shouldn't be here.

In the middle of the afternoon, Devil's Due looks just as dark and gloomy as the overcast day outside. Small lights dangle over the sparse tables, the wood paneled walls soaking up the illumination and reflecting nothing back. The front resembles a restaurant, with a dozen aging but orderly arranged tables and booths. There's a bar, but it's mostly a barrier between the restaurant floor and food prep area, and a significant chunk is a glass dessert display case with pies and cakes, all listed by ingredients and dietary restrictions. The deep red upholstery in the booths looks like it hasn't been replaced in Marcus's lifetime. Deeper in, Marcus sees a smaller, darker area toward the back, where the bar has stools for drinkers. The sound of pool balls smacking each other and laughter filters up to the front.

The walls boast a series of paintings of various pop icons halfway between irony and parody: the spokes-clown of a fast-food chain waving from the slopes of an impressionist painting of a mountain, for instance, or outlandish characters from eighties sci-fi movies imprinted on vinyl records set in rows. The bar itself is a sturdy thing of near-black wood with a thick lacquer, pocked and dinged with dozens of accidents and stains over the years.

A couple older guys look up at him from where they sit at the bar, then turn back to their conversation in the same smooth motion. Disheveled isn't quite the right word, but they seem faded, the way bar regulars can get after years. A trio of college kids—a guy and two girls—sit at one of the tables, eating burgers and fries and totally oblivious to anything outside their own little circle. Otherwise, the place seems pretty empty. According to the sign on the front door, it only just opened at 4 p.m., and it's 4:30 now.

What the hell are you doing? Marcus has no answer to that.

"Hey." A twenty-something with blue hair wearing a hoodie over a black T-shirt that says "I made a Deal with the Devil and all I got was this lousy t-shirt" nods to Marcus as she brings a fresh round of beers to the customers at the front. "Sit wherever."

She whisks away before Marcus can ask any questions.

A tall, good-looking bald guy wiping up the food prep area gives Marcus a nod. "Sup," he says.

"Hey." Marcus knows he really shouldn't be here.

"For one?" the guy asks, pulling out a menu.

"What?" Marcus winces. "Yeah, one—I mean, um, I'm kinda looking for someone."

"Cool." The guy hands him a menu. "You want a water or a soda or something?"

"Yeah. Pepsi? No ice?"

"Coke products."

"Ok."

Over by the bar, Marcus can now see into the darker back, where two dudes are playing pool. The balls crack sharply, setting Marcus's teeth on edge. They look up at him, and they aren't welcoming sort of expressions. They're pretty beefy, he realizes, and tries not to think about it.

Marcus knows he isn't supposed to be there. Following Lady Vengeance—of all people—after she hit him with that—her *fear thing.*

There was a thing, right?

Definitely a thing.

He hears her before he sees her. He knows that husky voice, below average for a woman, which sounds like she's smoked a pack a day for ten years. She sounds exactly like he has always imagined her sounding in the comic books he read since he was a kid. She leans out over the bar, into his field of vision, in order to whisper something to a patron sitting there. The man goes faintly pale and excuses himself with a grumble. He pushes past Marcus on his way toward the door, his eyes shifting from side to side. No "excuse me" or any sort of acknowledgement.

A moment later, the dudes at the pool table break out laughing, and Lady Vengeance cackles right along with them. The mirth lasts five or six seconds, then the guys just start glaring at Marcus in that forbidding way again. Great.

No problem, he tells himself. *Just—act casual.*

At the back, he sees an uproariously colorful music video playing soundlessly on a muted flatscreen. It's A-Girl, he realizes, in a series of increasingly salacious costumes and bizarre hairdos. In one scene, she's a schoolgirl with a short skirt and pig tails, and then she's some kind of snake charmer with a massive boa constrictor wrapped around her arms and shoulders. It's weird.

He heads toward the bar, very conscious of the tough guys appraising him. He makes an effort to unclench his hands, but no such luck. His collar feels clammy and tight, soaked with sweat. Is it hot in here? Maybe he should have taken off his coat at the front. Too late now.

Casual.

When he gets to the bar, Lady Vengeance isn't there. She must have gone into the kitchen for a second, and it's just him and the two pool guys, who come over to stand behind him. He can see their angry faces in the mirror, right over the shoulders of his gray coat. As a black man, he's been stared at by a quorum of square-jawed white dudes before, and he's not a fan of the "white supremacist or just regular white-guy racist" game. He tries and fails to ignore them, just as he tries and fails to ignore the sweat on his brow or how his glasses start fogging up.

Just—

Now the two guys step up to stand on either side of Marcus as he sits at the bar. He glances at one, then the other, and both say the same thing with their faces: "we will beat the living shit out of you." He knows what they're doing, and they know what they're doing, but nobody says anything. It's unfair, it's aggressive, and Marcus isn't sure what to do about it. He's not a fighter—not really—and while he could just get up and leave, that would make them win, and it would also cost him any chance of finding out about his father. And that—he isn't willing to give up on that.

"It's cool, guys," says a voice from behind the bar.

They head away without a word. Marcus watches them go in the mirror, then looks up at the dark-haired woman who steps out of the food prep area. Her hair is messy and uncombed, and either she favors really dark eye shadow, or she just hasn't slept well in years. In stark contrast to her pale brown skin, she wears all black, except for the words "Nasty Woman" scripted in white block letters on her t-shirt. She took off her jacket, and Marcus can't help looking at her muscular arms, seemingly sculpted out of wires and bone. A tattoo of a black vine with thorns winds around from her shirt sleeve down to her wrist. Marcus isn't great at judging drunkenness, but her heavy-lidded eyes and the slight sway of her step suggest she's a bit tipsy. That and the mostly empty bottle of Jack Daniels in her hand.

"He's just looking for a drink." She takes a swig of the whiskey. "This is a bar, after all."

She is also the most beautiful woman he has ever seen in real life. Or, at least, the comics made her gorgeous. Meeting her face to face, she seems ... why is he even thinking about this?

Because he grew up fantasizing about Lady Vengeance and her revealing black tights and low-cut top since he hit puberty, probably. Now—now it's just awkward.

"You're Lady Vengeance," he says. Putting that into words takes some effort. It's insane.

She looks at him levelly with the eyes of a murderer. "Vivienne," she says.

The tension rises between them, like static in the air before a storm. He keeps expecting lightning to lance from her eyes and stab him right in the gut. Or maybe, more realistically, she'll reach out at any second and put the fear powers whammy on him again, then walk away while zombies eat his brains. Maybe he should say something. Maybe he could, if she would stop staring at him with those wine-colored eyes of hers, like something out of a dream. He shivers.

"So." She leans against the bar toward him, staring him right in the eye. Her eyes are shockingly violet-red in hue. The comics got that right, at least. "What is it you want?"

"I—I want to know something," he says, stumbling over the words. "Something only you can—"

"To drink," she says. "What. Do you want. To drink."

"Oh." Marcus smiles stupidly, the tension easing. "Oh. I don't drink."

"No shit." She takes a swig off the bottle of whiskey.

Marcus grows suddenly nervous all over again. "I'm—I'm not even twenty-one."

She rolls her eyes. "Ok, bye now."

She pushes off the bar to walk away, and panic rises in him. "Wait!" he says. "I want to know about Justice."

Vivienne stops and looks back, her eyes baleful as she stares down her nose at him. His outburst startled her, and not in a good way. It's like just saying the name pissed her off.

Marcus tries to think of something to say, but nothing comes to mind.

Then she reaches under the bar and pulls out her clawed gauntlet, which she plunks onto the lacquered surface. The silver gleams, and the blades look sharp enough to cut through concrete.

"You want to be extremely fucking careful what you say next, kid," she says, her voice dark. Purple lightning seems to crackle in her eyes—her power, barely restrained.

Visions of the zombie attack rise in his mind, and his heart picks up the pace. "I don't want any trouble," he says. "I just—I just need to know about Justice. He's my father."

She stares at him with the same stormy expression, making his anxiety continue to rise. Then, when it's just about as high as it can be, and he's seriously considering bolting from the bar, her lips spread in a smile, and she lets loose an uproarious laugh. It's so sudden and so startling that all he can do is blink at her in surprise.

"Ha." She grins. "Ha ha! So you're the brat. Should've known."

Marcus can hardly think straight. "Uh?"

She grins maniacally. "Never could keep that thing in his tights."

"What?" he asks.

"Honestly." She takes another long pull of her Jack Daniels, finishing the bottle while Marcus watches, equal parts confused, impressed, and concerned.

"What are you talking about?" Marcus asked.

Her laugh peters out and she utters a long-suffering sigh. "Look, kid—"

"Orestes," he says. "Marcus Orestes."

"I didn't ask."

"Oh."

She looks at him in a sympathetic and somehow condescending way that makes him more than vaguely uncomfortable. Some of his least favorite teachers in middle school used to look at him like that. Like he was just not quite getting it, and probably never would, but it was endearing that he was trying.

"Look, kid," she says, idly adjusting a stack of glasses. "This whole 'find my parents' thing you've got going on. It's cute, but it's stupid. You're not going to find anything."

He's not really sure why he says it, but it slips out before he can stop himself. "I found *you.*"

Their eyes meet. Marcus expected Vivienne to look angry after that, but instead, she gives him a cold, calculating look that he remembers unsettlingly from the comics. It's like looking into the face of a particularly large, particularly angry guard dog. In the comics, usually she only makes that expression just before she really, really hurts someone. This is her thing—being intimidating—and it works just as well in real life as in the comics. Shit.

Just don't show her you're afraid, he tells himself. *Meet her gaze. Don't give in.*

Which is when he remembers that she's an empath, and she can tell when he's afraid whether he shows it or not. But maybe, he realizes, he just doesn't care.

The wine-colored eyes glitter at him, full of rippling power. "You're either really brave or really stupid," Lady Vengeance says. Worse, she slips her hand into the silver claw on the bar and flexes her long, sharp fingers. "You'd have to be, to come in here after what I did to you."

"That *was* you, wasn't it? With the fear thing."

Marcus clenches his hands. Rage builds within him, cracking all those walls he built around his heart that he didn't even know were there. The revelation of his birth mother, the guilt about ignoring the letter for so long, the truth about his father, the funeral—it's all too much. And now, to meet Vivienne, and have her stare at him

46

like that. Challenging him. Daring him. The skin over his fingers shivers as though by a static shock, and his muscles stand taut and firm. He needs to know. He needs the truth. He's never been so sure of anything.

Marcus opens his mouth to say something—beg her, threaten her, something—when the bald guy appears, a big glass of Coke in hand. "One Coke, no ice."

The bartender looks at Marcus, looks at Vivienne, then wanders off, humming cheerily to himself, completely oblivious.

The tension eases. Marcus breathes. Vivienne sighs.

"Look, kid—leave this alone." Idly, Vivienne turns his drink around in her claw fingers, which are far more dexterous than Marcus expected. "Shut your mouth. Drink your Coke. Go home. Get your degree. Find some cute girl or boy or whatever and live a happy fucking life."

Marcus clenches his fists so hard his nails bite into his palms. "Tell me about my father."

The smile vanishes and she looks pissed again. She closes her claw around the glass. "No."

Marcus's heart thunders. "Please."

"Fuck off."

In the mirror behind the bar, Marcus can see the guys over at the pool table staring at them. This is going really bad, but it doesn't matter. She has to tell him. She has to.

"*Please.*"

There's only rage on Vivienne's face now. She closes her hand around the glass of Coke with a faint hiss of metal on glass, and the top half falls to pieces in her grasp, fizzy cola running over the bar and dripping over the sides. She doesn't seem to care.

"Fuck," she says. "Off."

Marcus can't back down. "You *have* to tell me."

"Or what?" She starts to walk away.

That's when he reaches across the bar and seizes her arm. She blinks down at his hand on her elbow, more startled at his impertinence than genuinely upset. He looks up at her, heart racing so he can barely speak.

"You don't know what it's like," he says. "You don't know!"

Vivienne's eyes burn down at him. "That's right. Get mad. See if I give a fuck—"

47

"My whole world is a mess!" he shouts up at her. "You don't know a fucking thing about me and neither do I, and that's why you need to—"

Marcus realizes only too late that purple fire rings Vivienne's jet-black eyes, then ripples down her arm and up his hand. Where it touches him, his body erupts in stinging pain.

Oh.

Her power comes roaring out and goes right into him.

8. THE WELL OF ALL FEARS

He floats in a black sea, surrounded by blurry gray faces, all of them sneering or frowning or laughing at him. They look like hazy projections in smoke, rippling with the breeze and indistinct. He tries to speak, but his words don't have any sound. He has no voice here.

The faces speak to him, all in Lady Vengeance's voice, and he can barely comprehend anything in the ongoing babble. He picks out words—"Orestes" and "Justice" and "your father" and "wait—!" He hears bits of scripture. The preacher's voice at his birth mother's funeral. Bits and pieces of television shows. A-Girl's music video, repeating the same five seconds on a loop. He sees moments from the Devil's Due, each of which hangs in the air, stretching forever into the darkness. From outside himself, he sees himself grasping Lady Vengeance's arm—sees the frustration on his own face. He sees purple fire flaring in the air. He sees A-Girl beaming on the TV.

Faces loom over him, growing extremely large and far too close until they seem about to devour him. His mother. Athena. A-Girl. Lady Vengeance herself. Furious faces speaking with many terrible voices but one ringing condemnation.

"You," says his mother.

"Should," says Athena.

"Have," says A-Girl.

"Listened," says Lady Vengeance.

First he's starting with his birth mother—her withered, gray face unraveling before his eyes, maggots welling forth and flopping down like writhing tears. They're in a hospital room, but it looks

49

like no one has stood in this building in decades. Everything is moldering, black, and rotting.

"You should have listened," she says in a dark, low voice that doesn't match her lips. "I told you to leave it alone, and you just wouldn't."

He opens his mouth and forms words, but they make no sound. *Stop it!* he screams inside his head.

"Yeah," says that same voice—not hers. "No such luck."

Another face looms over him, and he's suddenly kneeling in a marble palace, its walls and pillars cracking in the embrace of creeping gray vines. Athena stands before him, not rotting like a zombie but beautiful and regal, shining with her own inner light. She might as well have stepped straight out of the comics: an ageless goddess. She is awful in the classic sense—filling him with awe and terror in equal measure—and sweat runs profusely down his face as he kneels under her judgment.

Her lips move, but the voice isn't hers. It's dark, rasping, and wryly sarcastic.

"I told you to fuck off, but you didn't," the voice says. Lady Vengeance's voice. "This is how my powers feel on full blast. Not very nice, is it?"

He tries to speak again but makes no sound. He can't even think.

Nnnnnnnnnnnnnn—

Now he's standing in a classroom. A specific classroom—Ms. Nguyen, AP English Literature, from his senior year at Roosevelt High. He's the only black kid in the class, just like in real life, and apparently his class is full of all the hot, popular kids at the school. Tough guy Dietrich Masterson, champion of the wrestling team, who constantly makes snide comments about Marcus playing basketball ("dribbling in your shorts") or tennis ("whacking fuzzy balls"). The super-hot Yumi Kujikawa, who dumped him for Lexi Davis, with whom she's making out right now. (And didn't his girlfriend leaving him for a girl do wonders for his reputation and pride.) Chet "Dickie" Richards, who beat him up every day on the playground in sixth grade and kept bullying him all through high school. Others who whispered racial slurs behind his back or when they thought he wasn't looking. There are a lot of them.

It doesn't matter that Yumi was the only one who was actually in this class, a year ago. They're all there, staring at him as though he's naked—no wait, he *is* naked, great. Even the campus lesbians take a break from kissing and fondling each other to point and laugh. High school sucked, but not like this. This has got to be a nightmare. This can't be—

Only now does Marcus realize what's happening. The comics call this power a "fear trap," where Lady Vengeance seizes a victim's fear and makes them face it in their own head. It's just— this isn't usually how the comics portray it. Lady Vengeance puts the whammy on a villain, and he quivers in fear and terror from nightmares only he can see. If the book shows the "fear world" inside the dude's head, it looks like some bizarre cartoon, not just like the real world except horrible.

This is like a dream. His dream. His fears.

His power.

A drum beats behind and around him. Once, then again, then again. Slowly it picks up a rhythm, like a deep, slow heartbeat, but not quite even. It's like a song. A song he recognizes ...

Shit.

Music swells: from the intercom, from all the devices in the room, from a band that has appeared over by Ms. Nguyen's desk. It's the first lick of a pop song—the one he dimly remembers seeing on the TV, and it's wormed its way into his head over the three weeks it's been out. He starts singing it in his head, but not in his own voice. In *hers.*

He turns, and there's A-Girl.

She's not wearing the Lolita get-up from the music video, but instead her costume: skintight white spandex with pink lines that really give her an amazing contour to her figure. The outfit doesn't overtly sexualize her, the way superhero costumes tend to do, unless she undoes a few buttons—which she has done. *Shit.*

No. This is wrong. He's got to stop this.

"Got a thing for A-Girl, huh?" Lady Vengeance's voice asks through A-Girl's mouth. "Hang on."

Purple fire—not the bright pink of A-Girl's actual powers— shimmers around her, and her white costume disappears, leaving her in a scanty pink bikini. Marcus has seen the billboards and awkwardly tried to avoid anyone noticing him looking. Part of him is going nuts right now, while another part is just getting more and more angry.

He doesn't even try to talk this time. He just thinks it. *No.*

"Tough break, kid," Lady Vengeance says. "But you really should have—"

With a strangled cry that actually makes noise, he lunges forward and wraps his hands around A-Girl's throat, choking off Lady Vengeance's words. She looks startled and her eyes bug out.

No, no, no, *NO!*

9. PARTY CRASHERS

When he comes back to himself, he's on his feet, leaning across the bar, hands on Vivienne's throat. A second ago, he was choking A-Girl, and staring down at Vivienne, she looks almost exactly the same, albeit with different coloration. The blonde hair has turned raven black, the bulging silvery eyes turned purple, and the face obviously older. In the mirror, the two tough dudes from the pool table are standing behind him, but they don't look tough. Their pale faces look *terrified*.

"A-Girl, huh?" Vivienne manages to gasp out. "Shit."

He's not dreaming. He's out.

"Let go?" she asks, her voice strangled.

Marcus still isn't sure what's happening. How did he make it out? What's going on?

Something cold and metallic taps against his cheek, and in the mirror, he sees Vivienne's clawed fingers resting on his cheek.

"Let go," she says again. "*Please.*"

He makes his fingers let go, and they back away from each other with a pair of relieved gasps.

Her bouncers loom up behind him, but Vivienne holds up her other hand to ward them off. A good thing, too, because Marcus has no doubt they would kick the *shit* out of him. She gives them a gruff little grunt, then waves her hand as if to dismiss them. Marcus is only dimly aware of anything other than his own hands, which tingle as though touching Vivienne scraped his skin. They feel raw—abraded—and not quite like his own hands. It's weird.

"I'm sorry," he says. "I don't—I don't know what happened."

"It's fine," she says, rubbing her neck. "My fault, really. I didn't mean to do that."

53

Marcus blinks. "What do you mean?"

Vivienne waves it off. "Got a thing for A-Girl, do you?"

"You ... what?"

"That was a full fear trap, and you used her to get out of it." Vivienne pulls down a fresh bottle of whiskey and pops off the top. "I only meant to scare you. Take what you're most afraid of and make it happen—provoke the fight or flight response. But I went too deep, and you went with fight. *Fuck*." She raises the bottle to her lips, not bothering with a glass, and eyes Marcus. "You've got powers, kid."

What?

"What?" Marcus looks at his hands, which are still tingling as though with tiny sparks of electricity. "No ... no I don't. I'm just a kid. I'm not even that brave—"

Vivienne nods and coughs into her hand. She's smiling faintly, like a teacher indulging a student who just doesn't get it. "Uh-uh," she says. "A normal human being couldn't break out like that. Not that easy. Whether it's some sort of psychic barrier or something that helps you solve riddles—"

She points at him with one clawed finger, making the gesture direct and accusatory.

"You have powers."

The moment stretches between them, and Marcus can't come up with something to say. All he can do is stare at her. He doesn't have powers. He's just some kid: an adopted orphan who barely knew his birth mother for like five minutes. And his birth father? Not at all. He came in here for answers, not some sort of showdown or whatever is going on.

And of course, the comics geek in him knows that this is *exactly* how it's supposed to go.

He's sweating. He feels light in the head, like the world is unraveling a little around him. His hand keeps tingling, and now his left eye is aching, too. Like he's got something stuck in it—an eyelash or a fleck of dust or something. He takes off his glasses to rub at his eye.

"I'm sorry," he says. "This—this was a mistake. I've gotta go—"

At that moment, a scream sounds from the front of the bar— not a playful scream or a startled "you just poked me" scream—but

54

something raw and visceral and inhuman. It takes Marcus a second to realize what the sound is, and it makes his whole body freeze up and a thousand little needles stab into his limbs. It's not the same as what he felt before: this is good old-fashioned fear.

Four people have entered Devil's Due, dressed all in flowy black clothes, like someone might wear for warm up before a wrestling tournament or a boxing match. Their bodies are beefy, and they've got the build of dudes who work out for function, not appearance. They're wearing masks that hide everything but their wide, angry eyes, and Marcus thinks at first they must be robbers or gangsters or something. Are those outfits some sort of costume? Halloween was months ago.

They look just weird and out of place, so he thinks maybe he's still dreaming, except one of them pulls a long, gleaming knife—a *sword*, Marcus realizes—out of one of the college kids he saw sitting up at the front and kicks the hapless guy down onto the floor.

Unperturbed, Vivienne leans across the bar to look toward the front.

"Great," she says. "Ninja."

"Nin—" Marcus starts to say, just as one starts moving a black-robed arm. Vivienne seizes him by the collar and, with surprising strength, hauls him bodily over the bar a split second before three four-pointed throwing knives sink into the wood. Two stick fast, like nails driven by an invisible hammer, while one rips free a chunk of lacquered wood and bounces up, cracks the mirror behind the bar, and clatters down onto the floor next to Marcus's foot.

"That's a fucking throwing star," Marcus says.

"Fucking *shuriken*, actually," Vivienne says. "But yes."

"What?" Marcus stares at the sharp weapon. "What the fuck?"

Vivienne seems pretty indifferent to his plight. She closes her eyes, her expression pained. "Friends of yours?"

There are more shouts that turn into terrified screams from the front.

"Um," Marcus says.

"Yeah." She raises her silver claw, around which purple lightning sparks. "That's what I thought."

Someone shouts, and the discharge of some sort of weapon thunders in the bar. A shotgun, Marcus thinks.

"Jesus *fuck!*" Marcus says. "Who are they? Fucking *ninjas?*"

"Ninja," Vivienne says, still concentrating. "Singular and plural. Like samurai."

"Ninja? As in—as in *ninja?*"

"Can't do a good fight without ninja, these days."

Marcus barely knows what to think. Somehow, he can still move, and he peeks over the bar. The tough guys from the back are trying to fight the ninja, but one gets cut almost in half while Marcus watches, blood rising around him like a fine mist. The other is already down. A ninja hurls more shuriken in his direction, and he barely ducks back before they stab into the bar and the wall. A bottle of vodka explodes and showers Marcus and Vivienne where they crouch behind the bar.

"Jesus," Marcus says. "Jesus Fucking Christ!"

"Everyone out?" Vivienne asks, eyes still closed.

"What?" Marcus shakes himself. "I didn't—"

But he did see. He remembers distinctly seeing no one else in the bar—the few patrons he saw before have vacated or, like the college girls at the front, are hiding under the tables. The regulars who were sitting at the bar have taken cover, one in the food prep area, one in the bathroom across the way. The bartender has a shotgun and he's taking cover behind the dessert case. Marcus saw three bodies: the college dude and the tough guys. How he got that much information from just a glance, he can't even begin to explain.

"They—they're all gone or—or *dead*," Marcus says. "What are you doing?"

"Working on it." Now her gauntlet glows with purple energy. It crackles around her hand and arm like living lightning.

Marcus's heart hammers, beating out of his chest. His vision starts turning a little hazy at the edges. Hyperventilating. He tries to wrestle the panic under control. He thinks about pressing himself harder back against the bar. He just wants to disappear.

"Can't—can't you do something?" Marcus asks. "You're a superhero!"

"Retired superhero," Vivienne says. "And I'm a little drunk, so be patient."

The sound of crackling glass makes Marcus's ears perk up. He can see movement in the broken mirror above the bar. The ninja are heading toward them, swords drawn.

"We are gonna die," Marcus says under his breath.

"Nah." Vivienne flashes a grin. "I love these guys."

They're close enough now that Marcus can hear them faintly hissing, like snakes. They move the same way, with sinuous, murderous grace, and if it weren't for the broken glass they step on, Marcus wouldn't even know they had physical bodies at all. They don't seem human. And yet, somehow, insanely, not only is Vivienne not afraid of them, but she's actually giggling. Maybe she's insane.

"You're fucking kidding me," Marcus says, more confused than afraid. "You *like* fighting ninja?"

"Yep."

Vivienne's power swirls around her face and body, down her arm to her free hand, where it resolves itself in a long katana of jet-black steel: a *fearsword*. Marcus has seen that in the comics, but in real life it fills him with a sudden dread that's totally different from the fear the ninja provoke. That's fear—it makes him want to run and/or hide—but looking at that black sword, forged out of pure terror, makes his bones ache in physical pain. That weapon is sorrow and loss and insanity-cracking horror.

Vivienne's eyes open and purple flame rushes out like tears. She grins.

"Oh yeah."

Without warning, she's up, vaulting the bar.

10. A BETTER WARRIOR

The kid's freaked out.

He doesn't, after all, run on fear like she does.

Lady Vengeance comes flying over the bar right at two ninja, black blade hacking high to low at the one on the right even as she catches the attack from the opposite direction with her claw. The razor-sharp steel screams and sparks off the blades of her gauntlet, and she carries her attack through to the slower one. The ninja's eyes widen slightly in surprise, and his body reacts faster than his mind processes the danger. She expected no less.

These men are warriors. Swordsmen trained to kill and kill well, with blade or fist.

But she is Vengeance, and fear is her weapon.

His blade comes up in a perfect block, but it doesn't matter. She hacks right through his sword, into the hollow between his neck and his shoulder, and it hacks down through his torso to his opposite hip. He falls back, broken sword falling through the air, blood welling in a fan. It spurts across her—into her face and mouth—but she's already flowing around toward the next ninja, who comes rushing up from behind them.

She takes their fear and molds it and makes it real.

She becomes their fear.

She drops low and sweeps her claw around, pulling the legs out from under the second ninja, and raises her fearsword to block the third: the one rushing toward her with an overhead strike. His sword scrapes along her weapon, screeching like a banshee caught between life and death. Faster than the ninja can get away, Lady Vengeance snaps out her claw and rakes him across the face, carving deep gouges into flesh and bone. He falls back, screaming.

And what do all warriors fear?

Lady Vengeance whirls to face the ninja she knocked down as he regains his feet, and they hold their swords at the ready. She smiles at him, her purple eyes manic to the point of madness. His eyes are wide and wild, fear rushing at his icy dam of control until it breaches and breaks open. She strikes just then, and he moves in response—just a split-second slower. They end up past each other, blades low.

They fear a better warrior.

Blood wells, and the ninja drops to one knee, drooling lifeblood, then topples to the floor. His sword, broken in half by the fearsword, falls apart next to him.

Lady Vengeance opens her eyes, her face sprayed with blood, one of the four-pointed shuriken in her clawed hand. She makes a mental note to thank the kid for charging her up with fear energy. He's really not a fighter, so the arrival of hardened murderers provoked a delicious fear reaction in him. It's been a while since she was around someone who was quite this afraid, and it's like offering an addict ten years sober a small mountain of cocaine.

Can't really blame her for getting a little giddy.

She reverses her fearsword and impales the last mobile ninja, who was rushing her from behind. The man's sword topples from his nerveless fingers. Not the better warrior, this guy.

"Yamero![1]" someone shouts behind her.

Lady Vengeance looks back over her shoulder. There, behind the bar, the fourth ninja holds Marcus hostage with a sword across his throat. He is standing up to his full height, every muscle stretched taut, and blood trickles down to pool in the hollow over his breastbone.

"You picked the wrong bar, friend." Her Japanese is a little rusty, probably, but it gets the point across. That and his buddy's corpse sliding off her fearsword. The weapon disintegrates into motes of purple light as soon as the body is clear, the energy dispersing into the air.

"I will kill him," the ninja says in heavily accented English.

"I doubt it," she replies in Japanese, though she's probably brutalizing the language.

---

[1] Translated from the Japanese: "stop it!" ~ Editor

She leans back against a table, her body language open and totally not fussed, and twirls the borrowed shuriken in her fingers. She looks at Marcus and sees something familiar. Feels the power in him. Fear, yes, but she can take that away. She starts absorbing it. Draining it. And what she finds underneath—but can she be sure?

"See what you have to do, kid?"

"What?" The word rattles between his clenched teeth.

She's sure.

"See it," she says. Not a question.

~

What. The Actual. Fuck.

Marcus's brain hasn't quite caught up with his adrenaline-fueled body. Following a woman he thought was a superhero/supervillain wasn't the best of ideas, but he had to do it. What's followed has been a goddamn nightmare straight out of a horror comic. It's all just too much: the fear trap, Vivienne going from bartender to ninja warrior/Miss Murder in seconds, and now there's an honest-to-God *ninja* holding a goddamn sword to his *neck*.

He's not all right. He's panicking. He's fucking insane.

So much fear bubbles up inside him he can barely think about anything else. The world is so loud and so blurry and disjointed that he hardly knows where he is. It actively *hurts* to try to make sense of it. It's all he can do not to start screaming or wet himself or collapse into a gibbering mass. The ninja grabs him, and Marcus just goes limp, hoping somehow he'll get out of this.

But Lady Vengeance's eyes lock onto his, and he has a chance to focus.

"See what you have to do, kid?" Vivienne—Lady Vengeance—asks.

"What?"

What is she even talking about? See? See what?

There's no doubt in her voice, and she looks perfectly calm. Like they just had a really nice dinner or saw a comedy show. *We've been friends for years*, that expression says. *It's ok. It's fine.*

And in a way, it does help. He feels the terror draining slowly away, replaced by clarity.

"Do you see it," she says.

It's not even really a question. She knows the answer.

What is she—?

He blinks at her, confused, then looks down.

He sees the ninja's foot, turned just slightly inward. He can't explain why it draws his attention—what about it distracts him—but he stares hard at that foot. Time seems to slow around them. Everything seemed to blur, the way light distorts around a semi's exhaust pipe, except for that foot. He sees it move without it actually moving. He sees how it *will* move—what will happen if he moves in a certain way.

Oh.

He steps away, really close along the blade but without cutting himself. He can feel the steel—its cold metallic edge, the wet blood from its previous victim, the extreme sharpness just a hair away from his skin. It doesn't cut him—doesn't even touch him. He just shifts past it.

And he moves so fast and so smoothly and so unexpectedly that Marcus takes the killer holding him hostage completely by surprise. The man gropes for him, his hand clenching hard on the sword, but before he can do anything else, he catches a shuriken with his face. He makes a sharp choking sound, his body going instantly stiff, and Marcus bites off a cry of alarm. He grabs the ninja's hand, trying hard to hold the blade away from him, as the ninja slowly sags to the floor. Finally the blade clatters to the floorboards.

Lady Vengeance, who stands stretched out after throwing the shuriken, exhales a smooth, deep breath. She rights herself, wavering a little bit, and gives him a faint smile.

Marcus and Lady Vengeance stare at each other in the ruins of the bar. Overturned tables and upset chairs litter the place, blood spatters the walls in places, and the corpses of ninja and a couple of the hapless patrons from before lay sprawled on the floor. Groans of pain and fear arise, and out of the corner of his eye, Marcus watches the tall bald guy come scurrying out from behind the bar and over to one of the wounded patrons. He's got a first aid kit in one hand and a shotgun in the other. He looks calm and competent, like he's done this a few times before.

"Cops are on their way, V," he says.

"Ok." She doesn't take her eyes off Marcus. "You with me, kid?"

Marcus blinks at her, blood oozing down his neck. Something hangs between them. Nothing romantic or sensual or even friendly, really, but a strong connection. Like the one that connects two people in a life-or-death situation. As that certainly was.

Jesus. He just saw how many people murdered?

"Hey." Lady Vengeance is standing on the other side of the bar, within arm's reach. She leans toward him, and her vivid purple eyes make Marcus ignore the blood on her face. "You all right?"

"Yeah," he says. And: "Fuck me."

"I thought so, about the sight." She leans back, a little relieved. "Powers, kid. Shit."

Marcus stares down at his hands, which tingle the way they did before Lady Vengeance caught him in her fear trap. He wants to dismiss the little blue sparks tingling around the fingers of his left hand as his imagination, but he knows they aren't.

"It's ok, Orestes," she says. "Relax."

"Marcus," he says.

"Yeah," she says. "But Orestes is a hero name."

"Fuck," he says under his breath.

"Hey." A cool pressure touches his cheek, and Orestes realizes Lady Vengeance has reached out and touched him. It should make him feel embarrassed, he thinks, but just at the moment, he feels comforted. Safe in a world seriously going sideways.

Shit. Now he's even thinking of himself by that name.

"It's ok," she says. "You're gonna be ok."

He looks up at her, and there's a genuine affection on her face. Friendly, warm, compassionate. The way he always imagined his mother might look at him and soothe him, back when he was a kid and had fantasies of having a mother. And sure enough, her touch—her words—relax him. It takes the edge off the thrumming adrenaline making the world jangled and crazy. He's suddenly seized by this insane desire to hug her—to *be* hugged.

It should be awkward, but somehow it isn't. He can tell that she feels what he feels, and though he's known her for about five minutes—half that time bloody and murder-filled—somehow she knows him more intimately than anyone he's ever known.

"Oi, keep it down, yeah?"

The thick, slurred voice comes from the front of the bar, where Orestes sees a gigantically huge man, rippling with muscle, his hands studded with thick brass knuckles. His accent is English, Orestes thinks—not prim and proper educated English, but something darker and rugged. *Street.*

"The best bit's about to start."

In one hand, he's programming something into a tiny piece of tech, and it takes Orestes a second to recognize a StarPod. It only looks small in the guy's hand, but in reality, it's bigger and more battered than any version he's ever seen. It lights up with a circle and starts playing music loudly into his earpiece.

The big man grins, and then starts singing.

Opera.

11. SCHEDULING

Her phone pings as A-Girl flies over the University of Washington, and she ignores it. It's her favorite part of Seattle to look at from above: architecturally interesting, classic brick construction, sprawling green stretches, lots of smiling people waving up at her.

Though ... mostly it's the tourists that point and wave and speculate as to what sort of flying object she might be. The college students tend to be too involved in their mobile phones to look up, and if they did, often they just roll their eyes and go on about their business in a very Seattleite way. Parker told her it just means she's one of them. Right.

Her phone sounds again, this time a full-blown call: the familiar ringtone she programmed for her agent. It's the most annoying boy band pop song A-Girl could think of. She did it as a joke, but he calls her often enough that it's starting to seem the joke is on her, not him.

A-Girl taps the little button on the underside of her helmet. "A is for Always Available," she says.

"Hey, that's a good one," her agent says. "Are you flying? You know I can't understand you when you're talking and flying. And it's dangerous."

"Dangerous to birds and tall buildings, you mean." In her flight, A-Girl swoops around the monument in the center of Red Square, delighting a few foreign visitors to campus. She flits through some aerial acrobatics, basically zipping around wildly for a while, making a little kid point in awe.

"Just land already."

A-Girl rolls her eyes. "Fine."

65

Wind whipping, she pulls up vertical and alights on the apex of one of the buildings. Or, more accurately, she bobbles the landing and puts a small crater in the roof. Any students who have classes in the upper floor of that building are probably even now wondering how it can thunder without rain. At least no one down in the square saw that.

"At least you're not moving around anymore," he says.

A-Girl bites off the sharp reply she was about to make. Of *course* he's tracking her phone. He is her agent, after all. Nothing creepy about that. *Right.*

"So what's up?" she asks.

Her agent replies with a long-suffering sigh. Parker Robbins is the sort of man of whom you just can't ask such an expansive question—not if you don't want a thorough lecture of an answer. She once asked him about his day and got a recitation of how many quarters he put into the laundry machine and at what times, and he probably would have told her the dates of each coin if she hadn't stopped him. Maybe today he'll get to the point.

"Angel—baby," he says. "Saw you on the news, and ... You've really got to think your appearances through a little more. Rehearse what you're going to say *before* you're on the spot. You know you go blank in front of the cameras, so it's important to have a script—"

This again. A-Girl rolls her eyes, puts her earpiece on mute, and leaps into the air, making the building shudder again.

As Parker drones on and on about public image and putting on a good face for the cameras—and maybe she should consider changing up her makeup tones, etc.—A-Girl flies north from the University, out over the Roosevelt neighborhood. It's this slow-burn tug-of-war between urban and suburban, with developers constantly on the prowl for deteriorating houses and long-time residents desperately clinging to their twenties to forties era houses. Every so often, a shiny new apartment complex goes in to take a faint sliver of an edge off Seattle's raging housing and rent crisis. There's a nice canyon park, though, and a big bridge over it connecting Roosevelt to Ravenna.

A-Girl doesn't know this neighborhood all that well. They shot her latest music video at Apex High School, on 12th and 67th or whatever, and by the end of the day, she was so done with

66

Roosevelt. Not to mention that Tom showed up, and they had an epic fight before she flew off in disgust. The paparazzi got some excellent shots of her flounce, but Parker managed to spin it into a rehearsal or something. Good old Parker. Annoying, boring, and intrusive, but at least he knows his job.

Her agent is still droning on in her ear when A-Girl sees a bunch of people run, screaming, west down one of the major cross streets in Roosevelt, heading toward the massive Whole Foods and the small shopping center it wears like a hat. It's just south of Apex High, and the panicked people careen through a bunch of students waiting for a bus. Bells go off in her head as she sees a bus approaching, yellow lights flashing.

A-Girl unmutes the phone for a second. "Parker, hey, call you back, ok? Bye-eee!"

"What? Are you flying again? Angel? Ang—"

She hangs up and streaks down toward the street. Sure enough, one of the kids gets elbowed off the sidewalk right into the path of the oncoming bus. He lies there, eyes going wider and wider, as the bus tries to brake in time.

Then A-Girl lands there and sets her shoulder against the bus. It smashes into her, glass shattering, the carriage caving in around her. The force drives her feet a few inches into the street, but sure enough, the bus groans to a halt. The kid—maybe a freshman or sophomore, it's unclear—looks up at her in confusion and terror.

A-Girl extracts herself from the ruined bus, pulls off her helmet, and grins at him. "Watch where you're going, handsome!" she says, and blows him a kiss.

Cameras flash from onlookers, some of whom cheer or freak out about seeing her in real life. More screams come from east down the road—65th—and the sound of crunching glass comes from a building just a block away. She leaps into the air, cracking the already damaged road again. Duty calls!

"Hey!" The bus driver pounds on the horn, producing an anemic bleat. "What was that?"

But A-Girl isn't listening. She's got evil to fight.

12. BOXING WHILE BLONDE

As the fist collides with her face, making blood and spit fly while her newly flaxen hair floats around her pert face, Lady Vengeance has one overriding thought.

Well, this is embarrassing.

She crashes to the ground, her cute pigtails bouncing, her adorable blue dress fluttering, and lies there groaning in a way that is anything but cute and adorable.

The Pugilist sings another line of his aria—something from *Barber of Seville*, maybe? No wait, she knows this one ... It's hard to tell just from the lyrics, and her hearing isn't too clear at the moment—and plants a massive fist studded with brass in her gut. The concussive effect is immediate and catastrophic: all her muscles lock up and her stomach compacts like a squeezed juice box. Good thing she didn't eat breakfast, or she'd be puking it all over.

She's sure she's had worse days, but she can't remember any at the moment.

As she kneels on the floor, gasping and choking, the Pugilist steps calmly around her, cracking his knuckles. He's hit her ten times now—maybe twelve—and she's drooling blood onto the floor. Orestes comes flying at him, flailing, and he catches the kid by the neck, picks him up, and casually tosses him against the wall behind the bar, where he collapses, groaning. He'll be no help.

Getting the fuck beat out of her by an asshole who won't stop singing. Great.

"Libiam ne' dolci fremiti che suscita l'amore—"

Definitely something Italian. She should know this ...

Lady Vengeance has been out of the game for a while, but even she's heard of the Pugilist. Never met him personally, but she knows him by reputation. Seven feet tall, four hundred pounds, built like a bull on two legs. Muscle for hire. Low-level enhanced strength and durability, just enough to make him really dangerous. The opera thing she didn't know, but it tracks. No shortage of weirdos in the world.

And if that weren't bad enough, she's *blonde*.

He deals her a rising uppercut that puts her flat on her back on one of the booth tables. It creaks under the impact, and her frilly blue dress catches on the splintered edges. This is going sideways.

Maybe it's the many years since Lady Vengeance last got serious about this heroism thing, but her powers aren't working right. She's supposed to assume the form of her enemy's worst fear; thus, against the ninjas, it made her a badass ninja warrior who was better than all of them combined. Against the Pugilist? It makes her every fairy tale heroine ever, but especially Alice in Wonderland. The outfit comes complete with a little woven basket, which currently lies upset on the ground. The Pugilist steps on a red, red apple, turning it to mush under his steel-toed boot.

This used to be her bar. Her home more than her apartment ever was. Just another total loss to write off.

The Pugilist picks her up by the frilly collar of her dress, letting blood and pieces of glass fall to the floor. The scattered traces of a fearsword swirl around her hand, but she doesn't have enough energy to pull them together into a usable weapon. The claw hangs loosely from her left hand, as she can barely lift her left arm.

"Libiamo, amore, amore fra i calici più caldi baci avrà—"

Is that just the baritone, or is he singing the soprano part too? *Respect.*

She's not sure what she's supposed to do here, and that's the shitty thing about the fear personification power. Sometimes it's obvious how the form is supposed to work—a superior warrior scares ninjas, a hockey-masked killer frightens co-eds, she's been the grim reaper a couple times, etc.—but what do you do when your enemy's worst fear is a cute little blonde girl with an improbably perky disposition?

You get beat up, is what you do.

The Pugilist lifts her up and crushes her against the ceiling, grinding her head back against the wood. Her bones start to tremble. Her head fills like it's going to explode. There's a heavy weight on her chest, even though it's her back that's up against the ceiling. She can't breathe. Collapsed lungs, maybe?

Dimly below her, she sees Orestes get back up and grab at the Pugilist's tree-trunk waist in an attempt to pull or push him or something. The big thug doesn't even notice.

The kid's trying. It's kind of sweet, really, but also ridiculous.

"Godiam! C'invita, c'invita un fervido—"

The Pugilist drags Lady Vengeance across the ceiling a few feet before tossing her into a wall, making vinyl art pieces rain around her. She crashes down into a table, every inch of her body in shock. She sits there, panting and bleeding and choking. Apparently, whatever about Alice in Wonderland scares this asshole, it doesn't involve getting beat the shit out of.

It's been a while since she was in a fight quite this brutal. Honestly, she doesn't miss it.

The Pugilist grabs Orestes's head in one meaty hand, holding his flailing fists away. Maybe it'll give Lady Vengeance a couple seconds to catch her breath.

Then he reaches across and wrenches her up by her blonde hair. *Nope.*

Lady Vengeance is airborne for half a second—just long enough to derive absolutely no enjoyment from the sensation—before she slams into the already broken mirror behind the bar. Bottles go scattering, including some of the high-end scotch. She ends up lying on the back counter, her head halfway in the sink, and the rest of the glass falls off the wall to rain around her.

All right, that was a good one.

She slips off the counter and lands on the floor, keeping her face out of the puddle of booze and glass and blood because her face happens to be propped up on her arm. There she lies, in the few seconds it'll take for the Pugilist to finish up with the kid and come get her, and tries to think of something to do. She needs a strategy, or they're both going to die here.

Where's Andre? She hopes he got out safe.

Lady Vengeance peeks over the bar to where the Pugilist is holding the kid up by one foot, singing to himself. Something operatic. He seems to have switched to a different aria. French, maybe? *Carmen*? She doesn't know opera that well.

Nope, she thinks. *I've got nothing.*

The kid thrashes and tries to hit the Pugilist, but he doesn't seem to care. The big man just tosses him aside like a bag of garbage, and thankfully he lands on the cushions of one of the booths.

We are definitely gonna die.

Then she sees it: the flaring pink-white light from the front of the bar.

Or.

13. LOVE PINK

A blazing pink comet bursts through the front windows of Devil's Due, shattering glass across the room, and streaks toward the Pugilist. Orestes sees Lady Vengeance's face over by the bar, lit with pink radiance and a maniacal grin. The big monster's face, equally lit up, looks stupefied. The flash moves faster than the sound, and Orestes only hears the explosion of shattering glass and cracking wood half a second later. There's a figure in the pink light, sailing forward like a bullet fired from a gun.

Orestes isn't sure how he's seeing this. It's like what happened when he saw the ninja's foot and realized how to move. The world has slowed for him, allowing him to see things in slow motion.

As the light gets closer, he can make out the image inside: a human figure, slim and wrapped in white that reflects the pink energy trail with dazzling brightness, making her hard to look at. Definitely a female form.

Oh my God. It's—

She lands just below the Pugilist and strikes with a rising uppercut, driving the big man into the air, his jaw and face tilting back. She puts out one hand to shove Orestes back and clear of danger. Then she leaps to the side, away from the bar, and propels herself like a rocket into the Pugilist again. There's incredible speed but no particular grace to the movement. It's like a flying tackle on a football field—a linebacker going for an unexpected sack of a quarterback who's not in the pocket. A human wrecking ball that's on fire. Uncoordinated, haphazard, brutal.

And effective.

They collide with a massive thunder crack, sending the Pugilist flying, trailing pink flame, to crash through the wall behind the bar over Lady Vengeance's head. At least she ducked.

The world rushes back to catch up with itself. Orestes blinks, trying to make sense of it all. Next to his head, he sees a long, high-heeled white boot wreathed in pink, sparkling energy. He looks up at a pink-striped, white racing helmet hanging from one white-gloved hand.

"You like hitting things, huh, Ass-hat?"

A-Girl stands over him, posed half like a supermodel, half like a conquering warrior princess. Without her helmet on, her long blonde hair floats on the winds of her own power nimbus, and the light makes her smolder. With one hand on her hip, holding her helmet, she points toward the Pugilist with her other hand in challenge.

"Try hitting *me*," she says.

The Pugilist makes a groaning sound but doesn't rise immediately to the challenge. A broken gadget of some kind is hooked on the shattered wall—an old generation StarPod. Orestes keeps watching the hole in the wall, expecting the Pugilist to come bursting out at any moment. Nothing happens, however, and nothing continues to happen until he realizes A-Girl is reaching down toward him.

"You all right, sir?" she asks.

Sir? Shit. She means him.

"Um."

He takes her proffered hand to help him up, or at least he attempts to. He misses her hand a couple times, though whether it's because of the shock of nearly dying or because her eyes are so amazing, he can't rightly say. Both?

God, it's really her.

"What's the matter?" A-Girl gives him a confused look. "Do you feel all right? Did you hit your head? Head trauma's no joke."

Say something!

"Fine," he says. "I'm fine."

"That's a relief." A-Girl smiles, even as the shadow of the Pugilist rises behind her, his huge muscles rippling. "You don't sound too sure. Are you—?"

As the Pugilist winds back a fist, Orestes opens his mouth but can't quite speak. He manages to point and make sort of a choking noise that almost sounds like the word "Look—"

As the Pugilist charges, A-Girl dips low and slams her two hands joined together in an uppercut into the big man's jaw. With a grunt he leaves the floor, crashes into and through the ceiling, then up through the roof and out into the cloudy sky. Orestes can see a clear hole through the building.

"—Out," he says. "Look out."

A-Girl puts her hands on her hips and joins him in looking upward. "Well then," she says. "That takes care of that, doesn't it?"

"Uh." Orestes is still staring. "Yeah."

Apparently, A-Girl punched the Pugilist so hard he broke free of the building and possibly the atmosphere. Jesus, how strong *is* this girl? Woman, *woman*—Orestes corrects himself. She's only sixteen, according to Wikipedia, but still. A sudden pop like a gunshot makes him flinch, but it's just a pink bubble she's blown out of chewing gum. They look at one another, and she smiles.

"What?" she asks.

Holy crap, what is he supposed to say?

Apparently nothing, because he just stands there staring at her.

"Angel," she says.

"Huh?" Orestes is lost.

"That's my name—unless you want to call me A-Girl. And you are?"

"Oh. Um. Orestes." He coughs. "I mean Marcus. Marcus Orestes."

A-Girl pats at herself, making gray dust rain from her white costume. She looks surprisingly calm, as if she's just trying to brush off lint—which is weird considering the wreck they just made of the bar. Or having punched a guy into orbit. Jesus, she didn't just punch a man into orbit, did she? How is this his life?

"Well then, Marcus Orestes," she says, holding out her arm. "Wanna help me get some of this off? Lot of dust in the ceiling."

"Oh, uh, sure."

Tentatively, he pats at her arm while she adjusts her hair. "Ugh," she says. "That's the last time I smash a bad guy through a wall without my helmet. Yuck." She coughs. "That's what it's for, you know."

"What?"

"The helmet," she says. "To protect my hair and makeup. I am bulletproof, after all."

"Oh. Right."

A loud bang draws Orestes's attention, and he sees the high shelf of liquor has finally given way and fallen behind the bar. The place is an absolute mess, like a construction site paused halfway through the demolition stage. The tables lie in pieces, blood spatters the walls, and he sees several drywall craters roughly the size of a human body. He finds himself stupidly wondering whether Vivienne should try to fix it up or just tear the whole place down.

"So you're just some random guy?" A-Girl asks. "Trying to wrestle the big bad?"

"What?"

"That's really nice of you, but you should leave this to the pros." That sounds rehearsed, like maybe she's given this speech before. The sort of speech cops give to wannabe good guys with guns. Those who didn't get killed in the police action anyway.

"Yeah," he says. "I mean no."

She looks at him, as though legitimately interested in him for the first time. She also looks like she doesn't believe him for a second. She arches one perfect eyebrow. "No?"

"Yeah," he says. "I mean, I'm not just some rando. I have powers."

She purses her lips. "You have powers."

"Sure."

Again with the eyebrow. "Really?"

"What, you don't believe me?" Orestes's face feels warm.

"Ha!" A-Girl covers her mouth with one hand. "Sorry. You just don't seem the type."

Now he's kind of offended. "What's *that* supposed to mean?"

A-Girl's eyes widen. "No, it's just—" Then she jerks upright with a little non-word sound, and her eyes roll upward in their sockets. Her legs turn to jelly, and she starts to fall over.

"What—?"

He catches her, or at least manages to support her a little as she slumps toward the floor. He knew that would happen, somehow, and that's the only reason he was able to react in time. Most people

76

don't just suddenly faint in the middle of a sentence and fall to the floor in a dead weight. Orestes isn't a strong guy, and supermodel-skinny A-Girl is a lot heavier than she looks—dense, like the difference between a manikin and a marble statue. He has to go down to one knee to support her, as if he started bench-pressing and the weight was just too much for him. At least no one saw that, right?

Wrong.

Lady Vengeance half-stands, half-crouches behind where A-Girl stood, her bare hand extended toward them. She looks really worn out, her face drawn in long lines of frustration and bone-weariness, but the gleam in her eyes is pure determination. Little purple and black lightning bolts flicker around her hand and up her arm where she must have touched A-Girl's leg or something ... Oh God.

Orestes looks down at A-Girl in his arms and swears under his breath. Her eyes have rolled back in her head, and she makes these wordless murmuring sounds he can only vaguely understand.

"What the hell?" he asks, not sure who's supposed to answer.

Lady Vengeance sighs. A-Girl half-curls up into a ball and starts whimpering. Her body shakes.

"What did you just do?" That was more of a demand than he intended, and he didn't realize he was so angry. "That was your fear trap thing, wasn't it? Why the fuck would you do that—?"

"Relax, she'll be fine in a minute." Lady Vengeance droops and almost falls over. "C'mon. I'm going to bleed to death internally here."

"She's ... she's Athena's daughter, right? Athena's your sister, so she's ... she's your niece, right?" Orestes asks. "Oh Jesus Christ, what the *fuck*."

"We don't have time for this." With a sigh, Lady Vengeance limps over to the bar and fishes through the ruin for some bottles. Bourbon, tequila, one bottle of scotch ... "In ninety seconds, she's going to snap out of it and be pretty damn pissed. And we should be as far away as possible when that happens."

A-Girl whimpers something, and Orestes's body tingles all over. This is really weird, holding her like this: like she's a lost child, and he's protecting her. Which is the opposite of reality, considering she can bench-press a tank and he ... what *can* he do?

This.

"I'm not leaving her," he says.

"Ugh." Lady Vengeance heads back over to him, with a pronounced limp in her step. Her claws grasp him under the chin to raise his head, and their eyes meet. "Come if you want to know about Justice—or don't. It's all the same to me."

She releases him, the metal scraping his chin like a straight razor, and starts limping off.

A-Girl's eyes squeeze tightly shut and tears run down her cheeks. She whispers something he can only faintly hear. "Don't leave me ... please."

Orestes's voice trembles. "What?"

Her eyes move rapidly under her pink eyelids. "Don't leave me alone like this."

Orestes's heart leaps.

~

When he follows Vivienne back out into the parking lot, he finds her in the driver's seat of a red sportscar, wires spooling out onto her lap. Whatever she's doing, she seems to know how, and her claws move in quick, efficient flicks. There's blood on her chin, running down from her mouth, and she wipes it away with the back of her other hand.

"You made it," she says, sweat pooling on her brow. "Yay."

Feeling profoundly shitty, Orestes walks up to the driver's side door. "This isn't your car, is it?"

"Oh God no." Vivienne bites her lip and makes wires spark against each other. "Not my style."

Orestes looks back at the door to the ruined bar. "This isn't right," he says. "Leaving her like this. She begged me."

The ignition makes a whining sound but doesn't start. Vivienne makes a frustrated growling sort of sound and tries again. "That was just the fear talking."

"Fear?" Orestes blinks at her. "What do you mean?"

"Loneliness," Vivienne says with a wheeze. "Very ... acute. Enough to put her out just long enough for us to get the hell outta dodge." The ignition sparks. "C'mon, motherf ..."

"Still a fucked up thing to do to your niece."

"Last time I saw her, it did not go well." Again, a spark, and the engine turns over with a growl and the car starts humming. "Fucking finally." She twists the wires apart. "You know how to drive stick?"

"Um, sure?" Orestes is still trying to put it all together.

"Good." With visible effort, Vivienne moves over to the passenger seat. "You're driving."

"Wait, what?"

Vivienne starts to speak, then hisses and tenses up. Blood trickles down her chin.

"Our—" She wheezes. "Our musical friend ... back there ... broke a couple—nhh." She flinches in pain. "Broke a couple of my ribs ... and ... and punctured a lung, I think." She coughs, spitting up more blood. "I figure I have maybe five minutes before I go into shock."

"God." Orestes freezes up. "I—I didn't realize—"

"Less talk, more drive."

He climbs into the car, and Vivienne curls up in the passenger seat. She coughs, and it looks like it hurts a lot. She's fumbling in her purse for something between the three bottles.

"I'll take you to a hospital," he says. "The UW Medical Center is closest—"

"Not—not hospital," she says. "Head for I-5 south."

In her bare right hand, she holds a shaking business card out toward him. There's an address printed on it, for BF Industrial. It looks like an old card, well worn, the edges crumbling. There's a symbol on the card, Orestes realizes: like a V made of two wings. It seems vaguely familiar, and he gets that same weird sense that it's important, but he can't quite place it.

"Here." She coughs, and blood spatters the card. "Take me here."

"That—that's in SoDo," he says. "That's like twenty minutes—"

She leans back in the seat with a groan and screws the lid off the bottle of scotch. "Better drive fast, then."

14. ALL BY MYSELF

At the bottom of the deep, deep well, the faint circle of light far above seems forever out of reach. Water drips down into the darkness, like rain from a gray sky just starting to open up. It falls, glistening faintly as it descends, into an otherwise completely dark place, devoid of anyone or anything.

Alone.

The word echoes along the rounded walls of the well, down into the darkness where she lies, curled into a fetal ball. She clenches her eyes closed and holds her hands over her forehead. The water falls on her blotchy auburn hair with thunderous sound that makes her shiver.

There's no one else. There could be no one else. Just her. All alone.

"Where am I?" she asks, though her voice makes no sound in the deafening silence.

You're always alone, aren't you?

The words without a voice echo in the darkness and her head.

"What's going on?" she asks, though again, she makes no sound.

And she already knows the answer.

Her body feels weak. Detached. The strength that carried her through the skies—that punched a man the size of a rhinoceros through a solid brick wall—has all drained away. She's a child again. Alone.

Helpless.

Abandoned.

Unwanted.

Tears well in her eyes.

"Stop that," she says silently. "Figure a way out of here. There's got to be a way out."

Don't bother, the echoing voice says. A feminine voice. *There is no way out.*

The words are like physical pain, but the light seems a little bit closer. Maybe there's hope.

"This isn't real," she says without speaking. "It's all in my head."

You just keep telling yourself that.

Angel—because that's who she is, Angel—squeezes her eyes tight, willing this all to go away.

"I'll open my eyes, and they'll be there," she says silently.

Doubt it.

She grinds the butts of her palms into her eyes. "Yes, they will," she says. "They'll be there."

But there's no one there.

Angel loosens her eyes a little, now she could just open them without effort. She purses her lips in a faint smile. "If there's no one there," she says, and this time she has a voice. It echoes in the dark, strong and sure of itself. "Then who are you?"

The voice makes a whispering sound, like wind through aspen leaves.

Pink light surrounds Angel as she lies there, and she slowly opens her eyes.

~

The first thing A-Girl sees as she opens her eyes are the broken remains of a chair lying on the floor just in front of her face. She blinks, taking in the contours of the wood, the angry yellowish splintered flesh of the chair's legs. She sits up and looks around. The rest of the place isn't in much better shape.

Pink light sparks around her and turns into flowing flame.

"That bitch," she says.

Then she takes off, leaving a crater in the creaking floorboards, and shoots out the hole she bashed in the ceiling.

15. GUIDANCE COUNSELING

What a day.

Staring at the phone, waiting for an update, Professor Frederick Francis can barely contain himself. The nervous energy makes his feet dance under his desk, and he can't even properly focus on the porn on his computer, let alone make any progress on grading papers or writing his own. This afternoon was supposed to be his time to work on his book, *Capes and Whips: Modern Myths and their Impact on Modern Sexual Expression*, but so many thoughts rush through his mind that he can't put together a coherent sentence. He's read the titles off every spine of every book in his office some five times in the last half hour waiting for the phone to ring.

Finally, it gets to be too much, and he has to do something. He grabs his sandals and slips one on over his colorfully socked foot. He's got to get out there.

His Bluetooth beeps, and he almost falls out of his chair in his rush to tap the phone.

"Fred Francis," he says into the Bluetooth.

"Professor!" Marcus's voice crackles over the speakerphone. "Professor?"

Francis curses. "Shit! Hang on!" He always does this—pushes the button on the phone, which takes the call there, rather than on his earpiece.

"Professor?" Marcus sounds far away and impossible to make out. "Am I on speakerphone?"

Francis fumbles with the buttons, nearly hanging up on him— narrowly averted disaster—and finally switches the connection over to his Bluetooth. The sound that roars into his ear sounds like a cacophony of road noise and honking horns.

"Marcus, how goes?" he asks. "Did you find Lady Vengeance?"

"Shit!" Marcus shouts, not right into the phone. A horn honks. "Get out of the way!"

Francis leans forward and clutches the Bluetooth to his ear. Unnecessary force of habit. "Marcus?" he asks. "What's going on?"

~

Some miles away, Marcus speeds down I-5, weaving in and out of traffic as best he can. He knows how to drive, but mostly he takes the bus. He's grown up in Seattle all his life, and public transit—albeit a frustrating, incompetent, extremely inefficient version of it—is baked into him thanks to two very environmental dads. He wishes, just at the moment, that he played more racing games and fewer RPGs.

Stupid thought. Focus. Don't hit anyone.

He's got the phone clasped to his ear, blood all over his hand and dotting his shirt and cheek. The phone keeps slipping, and he has to adjust his grip constantly. His heartbeat thunders in his head.

"I'm—oh God—I'm in the car with her," Marcus says. "And, uh, I think she's bleeding to death."

"Wait, what?" The voice on the phone sounds suddenly cold. "What are you talking about?"

"Heh." Incredibly pale, Lady Vengeance lies in the passenger seat, cuddled around her middle. Blood runs down her mouth and neck, and with her eyes half-closed, she looks on the verge of falling asleep. "Tell him about the massive internal bleeding—"

Marcus has to shout over the road noise. Convertibles are great, but they're noisy. Also, he's freaking out, and his voice is naturally really loud at the moment. "She's dying, Professor!"

He zooms around a Prius pacing everyone from the fast lane, going briefly into the carpool lane. He winces at how close he came to hitting that sensible hybrid.

"My God—just—" Francis calms down. "Ok. Slow down. Tell me exactly what happened."

Marcus starts to shout back, but actually, that kinda worked to calm him. Maybe his body is just worn out of panic. The adrenaline eases, and he can breathe normally again.

Ok. He can do this.

84

"We were attacked," Marcus says. "By a giant guy, singing opera."

"Opera?"

"Hey," Vivienne says. "Did you mention the massive internal bleeding?"

"A StarPod or something," Marcus says. "I don't know! He showed up and attacked V, and she turned into Alice in Wonderland—"

"Alice in Wonderland?"

Marcus bites his lip. "Yes! I don't know!"

Shit. The panic is coming back. He stuffs it down.

He really shouldn't be driving and talking on the phone. It's both illegal and dangerous. But then, so is hanging out with Lady "Grand Theft Auto" here. He checks his mirrors, looking for flashing lights. He wasn't a criminal this morning.

Oh God.

Electronic beeps come through the phone. "Professor?" Marcus asks.

"Try to calm down," Francis says. "Tell me where you are. I'm calling 911 right now—"

"No!" Marcus swerves to avoid a smaller car and finds himself driving on the shoulder. There's some kind of traffic jam. Maybe an accident?

"No?"

"She said no cops," Marcus says. "No hospital. She's having me take her to this place—"

"Place?" There's a loud fumbling sound. "What place? What's the address?"

"Just a second." Orestes looks at his phone, but he can't click through to find the address it's directing him to, so he opts for the blood-spattered card he stuffed in the center console. "1052 and a half? What kind of an address is this? It's on this card with this weird bird symbol and—"

"Raven—" Vivienne coughs. "It's a raven, actually—"

A chill passes through Orestes. "Oh my God."

"What?" Francis asks. "Marcus, talk to me."

"It's The Raven," Marcus says. "It's his symbol."

~

Francis pauses, one sandal on, the other caught on his big toe, his arms tangled in his coat. He suddenly can't breathe. This is real. It's really happening.

He leans over the phone on the desk, even though he's speaking into the earpiece.

"Marcus," he says, barely able to restrain himself. "Just go there, all right."

"What?" Orestes asks. "Is that a good ide—?"

"Go there, and call me when you get there," Francis says. "I'll be there as soon as I can."

"What? But shouldn't—"

Francis clicks the big red button on the phone, and a series of sounds falling in pitch sound as the call ends. He smiles widely as he finishes slipping into his jacket. He knows exactly what to do.

He picks up the phone again and starts dialing.

16. SAFE HARBOR

Orestes pulls the phone down and stares at the screen, which says "call ended."

"Right here," Vivienne says, pointing vaguely. "Turn right."

"Shit!"

Orestes swerves through traffic to make the exit toward I-90. His phone navigation is giving him vague, contradictory information about when to keep left, when to keep right, etc. He's only driven this way once—in his dad's VW bug, back when he had his learner's permit—and he remembers this section of I-5 having lots of exits in all different directions. His phone seems happy thus far, and he manages to get into the right lane, where the traffic slows down a little. There isn't as much tension any more.

"Hey," he says to Vivienne. "You still awake? Hey. Stay awake."

"It's fine," she says. "I can go to sleep. I'm not any more or less likely to bleed out while I'm resting. Common—" She yawns, making her wince. "Common misconception."

"Oh, great," Orestes says. "That's reassuring."

He takes the exit toward Airport Way and nearly plows through a red light. He only realized he should stop because of the massive semi heading through the intersection. There Orestes sits, trembling, clenching the steering wheel. The anxiety is coming back, hard, and he clenches his jaw so tightly his teeth start to ache. His eyes go to the mirror, and he scans for cops on their trail. Looks clear.

"Hey."

Orestes feels pressure on his arm, and realizes Vivienne is leaning against him.

"Do me a favor, all right," she says. "Keep talking to me. So I stay awake."

"I thought you said you could go to sleep, and it'd be ok," he says.

"I think—I think I have a concussion." Vivienne splays out her claws over her face, narrowly avoiding cutting herself. "Totally different. Talk."

"Ok." Orestes looks up at the red light, then down at the directions, which are telling him to turn left. He puts on his blinker, belatedly. "What ... What about?"

"Mmf." She nuzzles his arm until he lifts it, then she snuggles in against him in a way that might be really exciting if she weren't also critically wounded. She looks pale as two-week old eggs, and not the organic kind. "Drive. Push the speed limit but don't draw attention. Ask me about Justice."

Orestes swallows his doubts. The light turns green, and he turns smoothly. The speed limit sign says thirty-five, so he drives about thirty-eight. He's got to get her wherever they're going soon.

"Ask," she says again. "I might be dead later."

Justice. His father. Shit.

"Is—" Orestes licks his lips, which have gone suddenly dry. "Is he still alive?"

"Um." She frowns. "Ask me something else."

"Ok, uh," Orestes says. "What about Athena? Or the others in Supergroup? Are any of them—?"

"Something not about death, please. Trying not to think too much about it."

"Ok, cool. Fair enough. Right."

Orestes stops at another light and works on keeping his breathing steady. Driving slowly like this has allowed him to calm down, and now he mostly feels tired. Like his body could only manage so much stress, and now it's shutting down. He very much wants to pull over and go to sleep, but if he does that, Vivienne is definitely dead.

When did he start thinking of her as *Vivienne*, rather than *Lady Vengeance*? Probably when she stopped doing superhero stuff and all but passed out in the car. That and leaning against his arm: cold, shivering, and in serious trouble. She seems very human, rather than heroic.

Orestes notices a little girl in the back of a SUV pulled up next to them at the light staring at him and the battered woman in the passenger seat of his convertible. He meets her eyes for a second, then looks pointedly at the road. The light turns green, and he all but peels out, accelerating way too fast through the intersection. He can feel the scrutiny even as they pull away, and it makes the back of his neck tingle uncomfortably.

"This place we're going," he says, changing topics. "It's Raven's, right?"

"Kind of," she says. "Supergroup safehouse. But yeah, I don't think—" She shivers and moans, then readjusts how she's sitting in the car "—I don't think anyone else but him has ever been there."

"Really?" Orestes bites his tongue. She's never even been there before? That's not good. "What will we find there?"

"Right now I'm just worried about getting in the door." Vivienne shrugs slightly and leans her head again against his shoulder. "Raven and I didn't part on the best terms."

"What happened?"

"He tried to kill me. I gouged his eye out. It was a whole thing."

"Oh." Orestes drives through another intersection, focusing very hard on the road ahead. If only these buildings were a little more interesting to look at. "That's, uh, cool. Cool."

Nothing like that ever happened in the comics, of course. He does remember about ten years ago, Supergroup ended its volume 1, and when volume 2 started up, it was a reboot, basically retelling the story in a new, more modern context. He never got into the reboot, though he did like Lady V as a goth emo girl and picked up some of her spinoff comics ... Shit, this isn't the time.

His phone dings and directs him to turn right in five hundred feet. He blows out a long breath.

Vivienne raises her bottle of Jack Daniels and takes a big swig. Only now does he realize he's driving with an open container—let alone alcohol in the car at all—and she's essentially pouring the booze on his crotch. Three things he very seriously assured his dads he would never do. Well, maybe not that third one, specifically.

"What's the alcohol for, by the way?" Orestes asks. "Is that really helpful?"

Vivienne winces. "Anesthetic."

She drinks more.

17. ROUND TWO

Well, that didn't go as planned.

The Pugilist winces as he shifts his posture, crouched at the corner of the roof of the six story Meego Apartments about a block from Devil's Due. It's a pretty new construction, built to combat Seattle's increasing housing crisis. The Pugilist isn't entirely sure how he ended up here, but the broken crenellation and bent exhaust vent suggests that he smashed through them. Some of the damage is even shaped like his body.

He inspects his StarPhone, its surface splintered from an impact. He keeps it in a pretty robust protective case to prevent incidental damage like this, but there's only so much one can do to make a skinny piece of tech survive being punched a hundred feet in the air through several walls and floors of a building.

That flying girl has a great arm.

A voice crackles over his Bluetooth, but it pops and skips, like a scratched CD. "Sorry, Boss," he says. "Say again?"

"You got—address."

The Pugilist nods. His left leg must have taken the hit, because there's a big bruise developing on his thigh, and the pain's taking a while to go away. He doesn't mind it too terribly. Rarely does anyone actually hurt him, and he savors the short amount of time it takes before his heightened metabolism and fast muscle tissue regeneration takes care of it. He wouldn't mind fighting the flying pink girl again.

"I can't hear you nod or shake your head, Pug. Verbalize."

"Yeah," he says. "Yeah, all right."

"Good dog."

A shadow passes over the roof and lingers over him, growing just a little bit larger as he watches. Not a bird. Not a plane ...

The phone's still speaking to him. "Get there as fast as you can and kill them—"

"Hi there," a perky voice says.

Then the Pugilist finds himself yanked up into the air, his earpiece falling, unattended, toward the roof. "Pug?" says the crackling voice. "Pug, are you there?"

Dusty hair streaming in the wind, pink energy burning around her, A-Girl hauls the massive bruiser up into the air. He dangles from his jacket grasped in one of her hands. His feet flail below him, as though he's taking giant steps on the street a hundred feet below.

"You remember me, right?" she asks, her perky voice steely with resolve. "I mean, how could you forget? I'm the girl who punched you through a wall. Multiple times."

The Pugilist hangs limp in A-Girl's grasp, but he starts humming to himself. Faintly, under his breath. It starts soft—even gentle—but grows.

"I'll make this real simple for you," A-Girl says. "Tell me where she went—where she took the kid—and I'll drop you off at the police. Don't tell me, and I won't aim that well."

The Pugilist says nothing—only hums a little louder. Building to a crescendo.

"What's the matter?" she says. "You speak English, right?"

The overture reaches a pivotal moment in his mind, and he lets the silence drag on for a second. Two. Three ...

"What?" A-Girl asks.

Then he sings a loud, mighty note as the overture bursts into furious power, and swings one meaty fist up toward A-Girl. She's so startled by the attack that she forgets to let go, and he smashes her right in the chest, knocking them both spinning.

They wrestle, and he climbs on top of her, one hand on her throat and the other wound back to punch full force. Her bright eyes look up at him, shocked.

~

Of all the things A-Girl might have expected the big bruiser to do, attacking her while they're ten stories up isn't on the list. But sure enough, his big fist smashes right into her face, snapping her head back and knocking her helmet sailing off into the air.

Instantly she lets go of him and staggers back through the air, spinning wildly, but he holds on. His legs wrap around her waist and lock, so he rides her like some kind of 'roided-out messenger bag with a jackhammer inside and proceeds to hit her several times in the face.

She thinks "several," because the hits come so fast and so hard that she's too dazed and confused to keep count. His arms pump like pistons in an engine pushing the red limit. It's like looking upward in a sudden rainstorm out of the sunny sky, except these clouds are shaped like two jackhammers stuck together. And British—maybe? It's hard to say. She spirals around, trying to shake him off, but he's like a monkey on a tree—or a gorilla. He hangs on and continues his assault.

And it hurts. Her skin explodes in wave after wave of heat, and her mouth waters and her nose fills with snot. One of the blows compresses her left eye, and sharp electric jolts stab into her head. The rest of her body jerks spasmodically, screaming at her brain, unclear on where all the pain is. *Do something*, she thinks, but she doesn't have the first idea what to do.

She lashes out at him, flailing wildly, but hits nothing but air. His head just suddenly isn't where she thought it was, rolling around her wild swing, and he punches her three more times for her trouble.

All the while, he's singing at the top of his lungs—something in a language she doesn't speak—and punctuating the words with punches. And elbows. And a headbutt or two.

It feels like an entire orchestra is beating the shit out of her.

Unable to think or react other than flying crazily, she realizes they're out over the water, heading south toward Seattle proper. If she could dislodge him, he'd fall into whatever body of water that is—Lake Washington? Puget Sound? She can never keep it straight. And who the fuck cares, because she's taking a pounding, and she can't get rid of him anyway.

She finally manages to get her arms up, crossed in front of her face, but he fakes out where he's going to punch, making her flinch, then lands a big hit right on her nose. Thank her mom for super-strength, or that hit would have driven her nose up into her brain. There are bones in the nose, right? She can't remember. Can't think. Her pink energy falters and flickers around her.

Do something!

Deep in her sweaty, bleary, pulse-racing confusion, something snaps inside A-Girl. Something simmering deep, deep inside her abruptly boils over and explodes in a rising roar of outrage and hate. She straightens out their flight, points her fist in one direction, and pushes herself with all she's got left right toward the nearest building. It's a massive office building—somewhere downtown? She's not even sure how they got here, but it doesn't matter. Even as he keeps punching up at her face, she grits her teeth and streaks right for it, trailing a thick cloud of pink exhaust.

Dimly she sees shocked faces in a big window, then they crash through.

A-Girl feels the dizzying impact—the world goes black for half a second—then keeps flying, concrete and glass tumbling all around her. She smashes into an interior wall, wood and concrete exploding, then hurtles through another room filled with blinking electronics and some kind of business meeting, then smashes through another wall. She smashes through no fewer than five walls, then bursts out the other side of the building. Somewhere along the way, the massive asshole fell off, and she can breathe a little again.

"Ow, ow, ow," she says.

Her whole body hurts. Her chest, neck, and especially her face are all one big pulse of pain. Her arms and back feel as tired as if she's lifted three semis in quick succession. She keeps trying to think, but nothing keeps happening. She flies erratically, twisting and turning in the air, generally south.

"Parker," she says. "Parker? Call Parker."

Nothing happens. Her blood-and-dust choked hair whips in her face, and she coughs. She doesn't have her helmet, and she lost her phone somewhere. Probably in the Puget Sound.

She doesn't know where to go. She's flying like she's drunk—collides with one of those big orange cranes, still strung with holiday lights, and the force of it makes her shake. The crane swings around about ninety degrees.

"C'mon, Angel," she says. "C'mon—"

Something vibrates down at her waist, and at first, she wonders if he punched her there and broke her hip. But no, it's a little flashing light on her utility belt. She wears the thing mostly for fashion reasons, to carry her phone, and occasionally if she needs a tampon or lipstick, but she doesn't even know what's in some of those pockets. She assumed Parker made her wear the belt because it makes her look more heroic. Some kind of tech?

She touches at the flashing light—it takes three attempts—and when she makes contact, a bunch of numbers and letters appears in flashing red. An address, she realizes—somewhere on Airport Way. The flashing is also getting faster as she flies south. They did a photo shoot down there last weekend, didn't they? She sort of knows where that is.

Without thinking about it too much, A-Girl starts flying that direction, following the light.

~

The Pugilist pulls himself out of a utility closet on the twenty-fourth floor of one of the skyscrapers downtown, while a couple of dust-spattered office workers look on. One of them frantically hits the up button to summon the elevator, staring at the huge man in mounting terror.

"Down, please," he says, straightening his suit jacket.

When no one pushes the button, he leans across and pushes it himself, making a woman yelp and scurry out of the way. The man who was pushing the up button stares at him, frozen in fear.

"Lend us your phone, mate?" the Pugilist asks. "Gots to make a call."

Lip trembling, the man hands over his mobile, unable to speak a word. A stain spreads on the front of his trousers.

The elevator dings—going down—and only the Pugilist gets on. One man, suitcase and coat in hand, helpfully says, "I'll take the next one."

"Cheers, mate," the Pugilist says.

The doors close and he dials with his fat fingers, then presses it to his ear.

"Boss," he says. "We got us a situation."

18. INTO THE DEEP END

Orestes pulls the stolen—stolen!—car into the little unmarked driveway down on Airport Way and lets the engine purr. He tries to turn the engine off, but slaps at the ignition three times before he realizes there's no key, and then it takes a full thirty seconds to remember that Vivienne hotwired it. Something sparks, and the engine whines to a halt. Did he do that? He doesn't even know, but it's a relief. His hands are shaking. Maybe that's why people gave him a wide berth on the road. He wasn't even aware of it. All he could think about was getting to this safehouse place.

Or at least, that's what he hopes it is. Mostly, it looks like any of a thousand undecorated, nameless industrial buildings in the lifeless corner of the greater Seattle area. He's been to a few places in SoDo—there are definitely living, breathing people there—but this isn't one of those places. It doesn't look like anyone has been in this building for years. He doesn't even see an entry door—just a big garage door secured with a rusty padlock. The most interesting thing to look at is a peeling mural advertising a taco place down the street, but he distinctly remembers seeing only a vacant lot at the corner it's pointing toward.

"We're here," he says. "But there's nothing here, V. Are you sure this is the place?"

No reply.

"V?"

He looks over and his breath catches. She's lying there, head lolling limply against the seat, her eyes vaguely about a third open. Her skin is chalk white and there's blood everywhere. He's never seen a dead body—not in real life anyway—but she looks pretty dead, or at least in significant distress.

"Shit!"

He has no idea what to do.

"Wake up!" He cups her face. "Wake up! Shit!"

She makes a sound: breath escaping her smeared black lips. Still alive, then. For now.

Heart thundering in his head, Orestes looks around, trying to think. His phone. He should call 911. This whole thing is ridiculous. Maybe an ambulance can get here in time—

Then his eye falls on the garage door, and he's not sure why, but it grabs his attention.

He remembers that moment with the ninja: how he saw more than he should have.

"Ok," he says. "Make with the seeing. Let's do this."

He stares at the garage door.

Nothing happens.

He continues to stare, squinting slightly.

Nothing continues to happen.

He did it before, he can do it again. Maybe he's not thinking hard enough. Not *seeing* hard enough. He focuses on the faded taco stand advertisement. A bean, really articulated—oblong and outlined in some sort of indented line. A bean that looks like some sort of button.

"Wait," he says. "What's—"

He's already pushing it.

The air trembles, and he hears a loud buzzing that immediately sets his teeth on edge. His head starts hurting, and he stumbles back from the wall, lights dancing around him that he must be imagining. But no, those are laser pointers converging on his chest, attached to two placements that have popped out of the wall to reveal gun turrets. Miniature *Gatling guns*.

"Speak passcode, please," says a mechanical voice.

"Gah, what?" Orestes can barely think.

"Negative entry: 'gack what' not valid," says the voice, surprisingly cheerful but also murderous. "Four attempts remain before account is terminated. Speak passcode, please."

The guns spin, and Orestes can't think. With the flash of light, he finds himself on his butt and hands, crab-walking back toward the car. The sentry guns track him.

"Sorry, I didn't quite hear that," the cheery voice says, sounding half-apologetic, half-threatening. "Acceptable languages: English, French, Greek, Italian, Japanese, Latin, Mandarin, Russian, or Spanish—Mexican or Castilian dialect. Speak passcode, please."

What's he supposed to say?

"I'm Marcus Orestes and there's been an accident and—"

"Negative entry: 'I'm Marcus Orestes and there's been an accident and' not valid," says the sentry voice. The laser sights converge over his chest. The guns start spinning. "Three attempts remain before account is terminated. Speak passcode, please."

"Um, wait—"

"Negative entry: 'um wait' not valid. Two attempts remain—"

He opens his mouth, but he's got nothing left to say. "Um—"

A black boot appears by his head, and he looks up, startled. There stands Vivienne, leaning against the wall, hugging one arm around her midsection.

"Vee-cee-en," she says, very clearly. "Raven three-point-four."

There's a pause, as they both stare at the garage door. Orestes hardly dares to breathe.

"Welcome, Lady Vengeance," the voice says, upbeat and pleasant. "And guest."

Three clicks sound, and the guns stop spinning, then retract. The garage door remains in place, but the mural beside it abruptly shivers, then pulls apart to reveal an entryway wide enough for a truck, where silvery lights immediately illumine the darkness.

Vivienne reaches down toward Orestes, and he almost takes her hand. Then he remembers her wound and pushes himself up on his own. He means to say something—to express his gratitude for her help, and that she isn't dead—but he's just so relieved all he can do is gape at her. She nods to him.

Then, putting her arm around his shoulders so she can lean on him, they make their way inside.

"Enjoy your stay, Lady Vengeance and guest," the mechanical voice says.

"Heh." Vivienne spits blood onto the ground. "Doubt it."

~

They head inside, and the wall closes behind them. From this direction, Orestes thinks it actually looks like a door—a hydraulic powered hatch more suited to an aircraft carrier or possibly a spaceship. He's never seen anything like it in real life, and his best points of reference are movies or video games. Not that he has much time to scrutinize the portal when he's busy helping Vivienne shuffle along.

"Hey," she says, her voice slurred and rasping. She almost sounds drunk, which she probably is, but there's also an undercurrent of obvious pain there. "Hey, it's gonna be fine. We just need—*hrk.*" She stops and coughs, leaving blood on her chin. "See the emergency path? The red marks? Follow that."

Orestes takes note of red marks like a dotted line—the kind that looks more like a series of short lines with narrow spaces between them. He's not sure what that's called and can't think clearly at the moment. They light up with red light, powered by some emergency generator that he hears whirring somewhere off in the building.

Look for the medbay. Right.

He focuses on following the track, hauling Vivienne along. She's heavier than she looks, but maybe that's because she's only half-conscious. It's awkward and doesn't feel at all heroic. His arm and shoulder strain, and he's got to focus on each step to keep from falling over. Good thing all those red lights illuminate the corridor.

The path takes them through a door that opens automatically into a big space, like a warehouse. The emergency lights come on gradually, flickering on in groups as long-inactive subroutines start up in response to the first entry in what must be years. Human-shaped figures loom out of the awakening darkness, but Orestes sees them for what they are: manikins draped in armored outfits, sealed in glass cases. Many of them are bare or half-stripped, weapons and gadgets obviously missing. They all look vaguely alike, presenting a dozen different iterations of The Raven's powered armor.

"This ... this is all Raven's stuff?" Orestes says.

"*The* Raven, you mean?"

"Right."

"Should be. It's his safehouse, after all. Warehouse? Whatever he calls it."

"Wow." Orestes can't help a little bit of wonder. "Is that the Mark 13? With the slipstream drone system?"

"Nerd." Vivienne chuckles. "Field-tested, villain-disapproved. Tony never really got it to work, though. Not—" She coughs. "—not well enough for actual combat. He got a burn scar on his ass for his trouble. Looks like a potato."

Her voice sounds dreamy and far away. They've been listing toward a rack of metal cupboards, and now she stumbles and slumps against them. Her weight crushes his arm against the metal doors, and he winces.

"Hey," he says. "Are you all right?"

"Heh, Jaccob, stop it," she says, her voice ragged and delirious. "That tickles."

"What?" Orestes asks.

"Like—like this—"

Whatever Vivienne meant to demonstrate, it doesn't happen. She just slips and slides to the floor, leaning heavily against a bank of shelves. A streak of blood appears over her shoulder.

"Hey, V?" Orestes says. "Hey, we can't stay here. C'mon."

She tries to laugh or maybe she just hiccups, then winces. "Marcus," she says. "Nah, it's ok. I can just rest here. Just a little nap—"

"Nope." Orestes can't let that happen. "All the nope. C'mon."

He hauls her up, and they keep moving. He's got to keep her talking. Not that he knows much about first aid, but there's something about keeping someone talking, right? If she goes to sleep, that'll be bad. And he's not sure he can carry her by himself.

"So tell me about The Raven," Orestes says. "You said you poked his eye out?"

"Gouged," she says, her tone mildly pedantic. "Like this."

Vivienne demonstrates a surprisingly easy flicking motion, which would be terrifying with the claw on her hand. It's the casualness that gets him—she might as well have been snapping her fingers.

"That's, um, awesome." Orestes's collar sticks to his neck. "We're not gonna meet him, are we?"

"God, I hope not. He swore he'd kill me if he ever saw me again. He's tried, too." She coughs, leaving spots of blood on the corrugated floor. "It's a whole thing."

They head past a whole rack of guns, ranging from blocky handguns to rifles to sci-fi hand cannons and pulse rifles that look too big for anyone to carry. Orestes doesn't know much about guns. His dads never exposed him to gun ownership and made it very clear they never intended him to hold one. He's only seen guns in real life on a cop's belt, and as a person of color growing up in America, he knows to stay away from cops as much as possible. Seeing these weapons reignites something inside him, from a youth spent reading comics about costumed adventurers with jetpacks and energy blasters before he grew up a little and realized that sort of fantasy wasn't for kids like him.

His gaze follows the line of the cabinets up to a semi-spherical glass and metal placement in the corner of the armory. Three green lights glow inside the device—a mechanism inside the glass swivels slightly. Some sort of camera, maybe? It looks more like a gun turret.

"Are those on?" Orestes asks. "Is someone watching us? The Raven?"

"Maybe." Vivienne takes a swig of liquor from the mostly empty bottle. "We got in the door, so I guess the asshole didn't program the defenses against me, so we've got time to get our shit and get gone. Guess he's busy with whatever he's doing up in Denver. Or whatever he's calling it these days."

"Valhalla, you mean?"

"Mmm."

Warily, Orestes looks back up at the camera. "But he could be watching us, right?"

"I guess he could cut into the feed anytime," Vivienne says. "Probably watch every room of this place if he wanted."

Orestes shudders. "That's creepy."

"He's kind of a creepy guy."

They pause at the door to the next room, where the emergency lights are still pointing them. Yellow lights flash, something buzzes, and the door swishes open on its own. Orestes adjusts Vivienne, who is getting heavier—she's helping out less—and steadies himself to move forward.

102

"Besides," she says. "It's not like he's just going to go check feeds for 1052."

19. THE ALL-SEER

Far away, in a dark room at the top of a tower that overlooks a similarly dark city, a green light comes to life on a bank of consoles that show twenty different camera feeds. The light starts blinking—slowly at first—then faster. A proximity alert.

One dark eye opens, framed by the gray pillows, and it takes only half a second before full awareness returns to it.

One of the forms in the bed stirs against the man's back, and a lithe feminine hand slides over an expanse of brown, muscular flesh. The touch, casual but affectionate, nearly stops the man from rising. Surely the alert can be ignored.

Then his earpiece blinks with blue light from the bedside table. That, his private number that only a handful of people—two of them in this bed, for instance—even know. That, he cannot ignore.

He sits up, shifting the woman curled up against his chest, who nestles her head in his lap instead, and puts in the earpiece. When he looks out the window at the brooding sunset over the Colorado badlands, shadow falls across half his face. The blue light illumines the other half, and his gray eye opens wide.

"Speak," Antonio DeSantes says into the earpiece.

The voice on the phone is rich and husky. "Go check the feeds for 1052."

The sound vibrates through him, and Antonio narrows his eye. He is not surprised, but merely cautious. "Identify yourself," he says.

"You don't know me?" There's a faint sound of mirth. "That you don't know must irk you."

His jaw tightens noticeably. "Identify yourself."

"You sound irked."

Antonio climbs out of the bed, extricating himself with grace and alacrity. One of the women in his bed utters a faint murmur of protest and snuggles closer to the other. He heads toward the bank of consoles. He's already forgotten them.

"You have ten seconds," he says.

"No, actually, I have thirty seconds," the voice says. "Unless my memory's fuzzy."

"You're using one of my untraceables."

"Yes," the voice says. "But the point is, check the feed for 1052. I think you'll see a familiar face."

Wordless, he sits down in his control seat, the metal cool against his bare back and thighs. He touches the blinking green light, and an image appears, traced in hard light in the air before him. He inspects the faces of the two hobbling figures, and a chill makes him sit up straight. Silently, he touches the hard-light display and several options, so that it duplicates into multiple views from different cameras. They limp down a long hallway hung with portraits of various people in colorful costumes, almost always of a suspicious aspect and often featuring horns and sinister masks. Supervillains.

The other cameras show much the same. The woman leaves a long streak of blood on the wall. The boy, he doesn't recognize. He estimates eighteen years old, African American, glasses—college student. Obvious distress suggesting latent mental illness. Anxiety. Depression? Unclear.

He selects the option for audio.

"—bunch of our old stuff," Vivienne Cain says. "Portraits of our rogue's gallery. See?"

She points to one of the portraits, of a metallic combat suit that resembles a bright pink carnivorous insect. He can't recall the name immediately, but he remembers the battle very clearly: the threshing claws at the end of long limbs, the leering, bulbous eyes that could project force beams ...

"Some kind of praying mantis?" the boy asks.

"The Man-Tiss, yeah," Cain replies. The voice is slightly distorted, and the computer is still running analysis, but he knows it's her. He just has to be sure. "Also a drummer. His first bank robbery was to buy a new drumkit. God, he was an asshole."

"He?" The boy looks surprised. "Sorry, I just assumed."

106

"You wouldn't be the first," she says. "Skinny guy, really tall, long fingers. He was into bugs."

"What happened to him?"

"Heart failure. Marfan's Syndrome."

"Oh God."

"Eh. He and the Aphid fought a bunch of times."

"The Aphid, like *the* Aphid?"

"Yeah, fuck that guy," Cain says. "Real creepy pervert. Way, way worse than he is in the comics."

They're shifting out of focus, so he selects another camera to keep them in view. They're almost through the hall of portraits.

"Think any of them hired that ... the Pugilist?"

"That Mike Tyson wannabe?" Cain shakes her head. "Doubt it. Most of these guys are way out of the game. Last I checked, half of them were in prison and the other half, well—The Raven got them."

"Got them?"

She nods and points to another one of the portraits, this of an angry looking man with a crimson rune emblazoned under his eye. "The Brand, burned alive."

Another, this of a man with multiple jagged saws attached to his head like mohawks. "Buzzsaw, decapitated on his own blades."

"Jesus."

"Mmhmm." She points to another portrait, this of a panicked-looking man in a white costume that looks vaguely like a rabbit. "The Moth, insane asylum—can you blame him, costume like that?"

She points at a couple more—one in a blue costume, the other a skull mask. "Boost—maximum security; same with Reaver. He was on *Dateline* a couple years ago. Yeah, he *is* that crazy in real life."

With a flick of his fingers, Antonio switches to another camera, watching the two as they approach the end of the hall.

Cain points to another portrait, this of a haggard looking figure—maybe sick or starving, nearly skeletal. "Revenant, dead or undead—can never really tell." Another pair, which depict a tall woman with a spear and a guy with entirely too much makeup. "Thruster, twenty-five to life; Laughing Man, three consecutive life sentences."

Antonio allows himself to smile slightly. As he inputs commands, he turns his head. "M. H."

The women are already up and about, pulling black clothes on. They'll be ready.

"Prepare the jet," he says.

On the hard-light screen, Cain and the boy pause outside the door at the end of the hall. He looks curious and has obviously asked her what's wrong. She shakes her head, but she's looking directly at the camera. It's like their eyes meet across all that distance, through the camera.

"This door?" he asks.

"Yeah, that's the one," she says.

He types the phrase "NEMESIS" on the hard-light keyboard, then presses execute.

20. WHAT COULD GO WRONG?

They make it all the way to the door at the end of a hall that says "Medical" in big fading red letters before all the strength goes out of Vivienne's legs again and the floor softens, becoming like gelatin. She finds herself thinking about that time with Leoparda in the Jell-O fight, and this feels a bit like that time, including the reduced blood flow to the brain.

Only when she finds herself wondering when Antonio put in the bouncy house does her rational mind claw its way back into control. Not because it's absurd to have trampoline floors in your superhero hideout—she's seen some shit—but because The Raven II has never allowed such a thing as "fun" in his very serious crimefighting idiom.

Her heart beats very loud and very slowly in her ears. Low blood pressure. Shit.

"Kid," she says. "I'm about to pass out."

"Hey," he says, trying to sound confident. He fiddles with the door. "Hey. Stay awake, ok?"

The anxiety rolls off him in waves, and she almost feels bad about gorging herself. Almost. She needs a drink and takes a swig of the whiskey. It sloshes, the bottle almost empty, and she starts seeing it as a kind of life meter. When she's out of booze, that's when she can die. Until then, at least she has whiskey.

She realizes Orestes said something else and she tries to focus on him. "Uh?" she asks.

Is it the alcohol, or is she just bleeding out? Both? *Both.*

Finally the door opens, and a rush of stale air that no one has breathed in at least a year rushes out over them. Dimly, Vivienne hears recyclers kick on. The whole installation has been coming

109

online gradually since they opened the doors. She just hopes the generator covered the refrigerators.

"You know I'm not a doctor, right?" he asks. "I won't know what to do."

"That's ok," she says, hoping she's not inadvertently lying.

They hobble inside as lights buzz on around them. The rows of incandescent bulbs light up away from them and around the chamber, filling the space with a cool blue light. One burns out and explodes with a loud burst, making all the nearby bulbs start flickering. Could be worse.

"There." She points to a table in the middle, with a number of machines hanging over it. She's always thought they look like robot arms holding laser guns, but at least they aren't saws and syringes.

She struggles out of her leather jacket, leaving it in a heap on the floor. What are a few more bloodstains? Orestes is looking at the device, which must resemble something out of a sci-fi movie.

"What is this?" he asks.

"Auto-laparoscopic processor," she says. "It's—"

"A surgery machine," Orestes says. "They had something like this in *Hot Vengeance* number 17—one of The Raven's, though it didn't look anything like this." He looks at her and flushes. "It's a comic book. Er, about you."

"I know what it is," she says. That's a pretty deep cut—that comic came out over ten years ago, back when they were still making those. Not that she got royalties. "Anyway, assuming it still has juice, and the meds haven't spoiled, the machine should do all the work. Help me—*unf.*"

She can't seem to climb up on it by herself, so Orestes extends his arms for her to lean on. She slips on half-numb legs and presses her chest into his, and looks up at him, eyes big.

"You've got to take my clothes off," she says.

"Wh-what?"

Their faces are really close together, and his cheeks deepen in color as she watches. The kid's definitely not a player, and she wouldn't be surprised if he has no sexual experience at all. All he knows about women, he probably got from movies. Not that she's helping right now. But it's just so fun, and she's dying so it's fine to tease him. Right?

"Kidding," she says. "Just my shirt. Ok?"

"Oh. Ok."

He does help her, studiously avoiding looking down. Taking off the shirt has got to be the most painful thing she's had to do for a while. Her whole middle rattles around inside her skin, barely fitting. Maybe she should have cut it off. That would have worked better, maybe. She has to drink the rest of the whiskey just to deal with it.

"Oh shit," he says. "That—that doesn't look good."

She checks out her torso, which looks like a sausage. She can tell more than one of her ribs is broken and/or dislocated, and she's definitely bleeding internally, if not much on the surface. Her stomach is hard to the touch—filling up with blood.

"Don't worry," she says. "This'll work."

"You sure?" Orestes asks. "No. Silly question. Of course you're sure."

"Of course I'm sure," she says.

She isn't sure.

She lies back on the entirely freezing table, which is an odd mixture of discomfort from the cold metal and relief because at least she's not on her feet. She touches her stomach and winces.

"Ready?" he asks.

"Hang on." Awkwardly, she makes sure the empty bottle ends up on the nearby counter. She can't help seeing it as an empty life meter. Shit.

"Over there," she says, nodding toward a set of controls.

He looks wary. "I told you I don't know what I'm doing."

"Tony made it idiot-proof. Just find the power button, then hit scan, then ok when it returns a diagnosis. The automated surgery should do the rest."

"What if it diagnoses the wrong condition?" Orestes asks.

"You mean, worse than we'd do on our own?"

"Right."

Orestes pushes the red power button, and the machine whirs to life. Immediately one of the arms starts passing a scanning light over her, like sending a fax. Vivienne turns her head to the side so she can look at him. He's standing by the machine, arms crossed. He's about to snap.

"Hey, kid?" she asks. "About the blushing thing. It's really cute."

111

"Oh." He eases a little. "Yeah?"

"Yes," she says. "But we've got more important things to worry about."

Like death, for instance, but she doesn't say that.

"Right," he says. "Sorry, this—this is just a little surreal."

"Sure," she says. "It'll be ok. Promise."

It works. He eases up a little, his anxiety shifting into reassurance. He's out of his depth, but he trusts her. That's good, because the room is getting really dizzy and weird. The Raven's medical bay.

The Raven, who profoundly hates her.

What could go wrong?

The machine finishes up its scan and starts whirring. Orestes hesitates at the panel, looking down at the readout. Her diagnosis, probably. He's saying something, but she can't understand what. It all sounds so far, far away. Less important. Nothing matters anymore.

She hears another, deeper voice, from deep down below. *Vivienne* ...

She wipes her mouth, and her fingers come away bloody. "Hey."

It must have been just a whisper, because he has to stoop down to hear her. She touches his cheek with her bloody fingers. The blue light makes his features luminous, and one of his eyes seems to be very dark, like it doesn't exist anymore. Weird. She should be seeing double, not halfsies.

"Don't freak out," she says. "But remember when I said I was going to pass out?"

"Yes?" Orestes says. "Are you going to—?"

The world stretches.

~

Her eyes close, her hand slips from his cheek, and she lies unmoving on the table.

"—pass out," Orestes says. "Crap."

He isn't sure if she fell asleep or died, and he doesn't even know how to check. He feels at her neck, adjusting his fingers several times, and he feels something moving there. A pulse.

The control panel beeps, and he sees one of the buttons gently flashing yellow to remind him the scan is complete and the surgery ready to go. He isn't sure how he knows that, but one look in that direction, and he understands. The same way he knew what to do when he activated it. Now he stands before the keyboard, trying to figure out what to do.

"C'mon," he says. "We got this."

The keys aren't even a normal QWERTY keyboard. Most of the keys are unmarked, and he doesn't recognize the symbols on the ones that have them. Maybe they're letters, but they look more like pictographs or hieroglyphs or who knows what. He's got no idea what to do.

A faint sound behind Orestes makes him look around. Vivienne starts shaking slightly.

"Come on!" he says. "Figure it out. Come on, powers. Work!"

He doesn't have time for this. Doesn't have time to wait.

That's when the alarm goes off, a senses-shattering blare like a fire alarm that induces epileptic seizures, and flashing red lights fill the facility. Orestes freezes up, startled and terrified, and all of a sudden, he knows exactly what keys to hit. He puts in a set of commands, the flashing button turns green, and he hits it. The machines over Vivienne whir to life and start projecting waves of energy at her.

"Nice," he says. "Ok. We got this."

Then the sentry bots appear, worming out of those semi-spherical placements at the corners of the rooms. They look like skill saws with tentacles and burning red eyes.

"Oh, come *on*!" Orestes says.

21. NEMESIS: EXECUTE

(This is the way it would go.)

"Robots," the ideal Orestes would say as the sentry bots come swarming toward him. "I hate robots the way most people hate ninja. And I hate ninja, too."

He'd stride out from cover and raise a sci-fi pulse rifle, unloading a stream of plasma bursts to disintegrate the nearest robots. A turret in the corner would wheel toward him, but he'd blast it before it could fire so its shots would go wild, carving an arc through the ceiling. Matrix-style, he'd swing behind a conveniently placed pillar as the other robots fired upon him, carving off chunks of metal and stone.

"But this time," he would say, his voice low and menacing. "This time, shit's *personal.*"

He'd risk a look over at Vivienne, who would still be being fixed up on the table. They wouldn't be attacking her, yet, but the second she moves ... *Gotta rescue her.*

He would sense the robot rolling out to flank him an instant before it started firing and know where to move. He'd dive from cover toward the operation table, where the machines would retract from Vivienne's mostly naked body, their work done. She'd stir, drawing the robots' attention. He'd blow two more out of the air, sending parts cascading, then leap up to land on the table in a crouch. The last sentry bot would blow the rifle out of his hands, but fine. Lightning would crackle around his fist, and he'd lunge upward with a cry to uppercut it, and it would smash into useless slag against the ceiling.

The explosion would make Vivienne's eyes fly wide open. "Marcus! What's happening?"

"Don't worry." He would smile and reach down with his free hand to help her up. "I got this."

She'd take his hand, then make a little *eep* sound. One of the spider-like drones would have scrambled up onto the surgical bed, obviously damaged but still trying to fulfill its purpose, and stabbed its little talon arms at her leg. Orestes would kick it flying, his foot not even hurting a little bit, then zap it out of the air with lightning from his fingertips.

"Nice!" Vivienne would grin wide and press herself against his side, clinging for balance. "You're so powerful. I had no idea."

"Oh yeah," he would say, or something suitably self-confident and cool like that. Maybe, "You know it, baby."

He would call her "baby," and it wouldn't be weird.

Then he'd lay down a storm of lightning to take out all the drones and turrets in the room.

Vivienne would look at him in a whole new way—her eyes slightly narrowed, biting her lower lip. Consideringly. "You know," she would say. "You're not *that* much younger than me—"

(Oh shit, she's about to kiss me.)

He'd be about to say something witty and charming when a strangled cry from the trophy room would draw their attention. "Orestes! Help!"

(Is that...?)

"A-Girl!" Orestes would leap off the table, do a superhero landing, and rush out into the hall.

There she would be, her white and pink skintight outfit scuffed and torn, surrounded by a dozen or more of the hunter killers. She'd be fending them off, but only sort of, like a girl on a stool batting futilely at a mouse in a fifties cartoon. She'd even be biting her nails.

"Oh, save me, Orestes!" she would cry.

(Of course she's here too.)

He would charge in, lightning rolling around him like something out of a summer blockbuster. He'd punch, kick, and blast, making robots explode or go inert all around him. A particularly nasty sentry with small laser blades projecting like knives from its tentacles might get right in his way and get in a lucky slash right across his rippling muscular chest. He would feel the pain faintly, but somehow, he would know the wound would be mostly just

116

cosmetic. Then he'd reply with blue laser beams that flare from his eyes and burn two neat holes through the creature.

(Sure. Eyebeams. Why not.)

He'd ride the lightning right up to A-Girl, who would wrap her arms around him and kiss him on the cheek. "My hero!" she would say.

"Nice moves, kid," Lady Vengeance would say. She'd suddenly be wearing her black leather costume, the one from *Vengeance Strikes Back #1*, with the cover that had to be pulled from comic shops when parents complained. She'd wrap her arms around his leg as he stood there heroically.

And why not? He would be the hero, the crackling lightning making him heroic. Mythic.

(Except.)

~

None of that happens, obviously.

Actual Orestes cowers behind one of the operation tables while the killer robots look for him. Red swaths of light sweep around the med-bay, scanning for movement and targets. Sweat streaks down his face, and the whirring sound of their operation makes him wince. He can see them dimly in the reflection on one of the storage cabinets against the wall: floating monstrosities of tentacles and whirring blades. And him without a weapon.

It's less *Terminator* and more *Jurassic Park*. You know, the kitchen scene.

What he wouldn't give for functioning powers that could actually help him here.

He really has to stop fantasizing so much. And maybe talk to his therapist about some deep-seated sexism, not to mention the mental lamp-shading. He doesn't really think about women in general, and those women in particular, that way, does he? *Shit.*

He risks a glance at Vivienne, who's still being fixed up, and the sentries immediately let loose with electric blasts that drive him back behind cover with a sharp intake of breath. The air burns and tingles, and he can smell something sharp and astringent. Is that what ozone smells like? He looks down at the ugly black mark the lightning painted across the floor, stretching jaggedly toward a supply cabinet against the far wall. The door has dented and popped open, spilling sealed vials that start rolling around the floor. Two vials come to a rest, one by one, by his left shoe. A couple break near the storage cabinet, and Orestes hears and smells the sizzling chemicals mixing. Great.

Some hero he is.

One of the sentry bots makes a whirring sound, and a red scanning light flicks over the small chemical reaction happening by the cabinet. It takes him a second, but Orestes understands: the robots are drawn to the sound and movement. In that case ...

Slowly, he picks up the vials, then chucks one as hard as he can through the open door to the hall. It smashes on the wall inside with a crinkle of glass.

Instantly, the approaching robots react, turning in that direction with inhuman speed. Their sensors click, multi-lens eyes focusing and refocusing. He can't tell much from the reflection in the cabinet, but at least they aren't immediately focusing on him. He risks a glance over the edge of the table, and they don't take his head off with an electrical discharge, so that's good. He throws the other vial, which bounces off the wall not far from where the first hit, cracks on the floor, and rolls.

That's enough. They lunge in that direction like fired bullets. They whir, spilling over themselves with efficient, mechanized movement that reminds Orestes of some nightmare combination of a snake and a spider. Orestes presses himself against the table, trying to rein in his heavy breathing.

He can do this. He can.

When the last of the robots is out of the medbay, Orestes edges along behind the tables and hurries over to the doors. The sentry bots keep scanning the corridor: six red laser spotlights dancing along every surface. Two of them are working on scanning the chemical spill, while the others search behind all of the display cases. One seems to have taken significant interest in Vivienne's blood trail on the wall.

Orestes reaches over to push the door handle, but the thing doesn't budge. Automatic, right. There's got to be some kind of manual override, but whatever power he used earlier isn't working, and in his panic, he can't figure it out. His heart thunders in his head, drowning out thought.

Back on the table, Vivienne makes a murmuring sound that makes Orestes go taut in surprise. One of the drones whirs, and its optics swivel. Shit.

He strains at the door for a second, but it won't budge. Shit. *Shit!*

The bot's sensors flash, and it points its emitter toward him. Blue electricity sparks, and Orestes can feel the air shiver. His hand finds an unseen lever and abruptly the door frees on its slide.

With a cry, Orestes slams it closed just as the drone fires at him. Electricity blasts the door, and he feels it like a concussive force that knocks him back—or maybe it's just his own sense of self-preservation. He lands on his backside on the floor, blinking, and sees the robot appear behind the ballistic glass.

"Ha!" he says. "Got you!"

Its angry red light shines down at him, and they consider one another for a moment that stretches. Then the door starts to move, and one of the robot's tentacles snakes through the gap between door and jamb.

Shit.

Orestes scrambles to his feet and slams the door shut again so hard his shoulder feels like he's pulling it apart. An ugly grinding sound of metal on metal announces the damage to the drone, though, and the end of its snaking tentacle flops down and twitches feebly just inside the door. Without even thinking, Orestes engages a manual lock, sealing the door. On the other side of the soundproof door, the robots bash against it with muted thuds, unable to get the door back open.

"Yeah!" Orestes says. "In your face!"

Something touches his arm from behind, and he freezes in sudden panic.

"Don't jinx it, kid," Vivienne says as she leans heavily against him. She's woozy, but she's on her feet. Which is pretty good for just having had surgery. "You say something like that, and shit is bound to happen."

Which is when the ceiling of the trophy hall abruptly collapses inward as something—*someone*—comes tumbling through. It's oddly silent, as the door blocks all but a faint rumble. Orestes has just enough time to see a flash of neon pink energy before dust fills the chamber, and then electricity starts flashing as the robots turn on the newcomer.

"What the sh——?" Orestes asks, but a hurled robot smashes into the glass, sending cracks through it. It tumbles free, and he sees A-Girl, her helmet missing, and her costume tattered and thoroughly smeared and scuffed with dust, amongst the drones. As he watches, she smashes one of the drones aside like an annoying fly, and it hurtles against the wall to smash with a dull *thump* into useless bits. Everything sounds muted through the soundproofing, but that must have been as loud as gunshot. She looks at them, enraged pink energy flowing from her eyes.

"Shit like that," Vivienne says, and winces. "C'mon."

"Wait——" Orestes tries to hold back, but she drags him across the med-bay toward another set of doors. Meanwhile, A-Girl keeps fighting the sentry robots, electricity crackling in a crazy light show through the ballistic glass. Vivienne half-escorts, half-drags him to the far wall and gets to work on the access panel there.

"You're already up?" Orestes asks. "That's amazing."

"Yeah, well, lots of painkillers, including my good friend Jack," she says, as the access pad flashes red and returns a loud sound of rejection. "No powers to speak of, and I can't even feel anything from you. Pretty goddamn sweet, honestly, but we're on a schedule."

She puts in another code, and again it's rejected. She mutters a curse and presses the heel of her hand over her left eye. "Oh, fuck *me.*"

A muted bang draws Orestes's attention back to the opposite door, where the crazy lights have stopped flashing. The door shudders under another blow, and this time it leaves a shallow impression in the solid steel. One that looks a bit like a foot.

"Can she——?" he asks, and winces with another blow. "Can she get through that?"

"Oh yeah." Vivienne puts in a third code, and hovers over the last number. "Seven or nine?"

"What?" Orestes asks.

"I've only got three chances before I'm locked out," she says. "I'm pretty sure on the first three numbers, and I think the fourth one is a seven or a nine. Pick one."

"What—what happens if we get it wrong?"

"Nerve gas, probably?" Vivienne says. "I dunno, it's The Raven, he's an asshole. Just *pick*."

Jesus.

Orestes looks at the panel, and he has absolutely no idea. Nothing about the numbers stands out. There aren't any thumbprints he can see, and he didn't hear any different tones when Vivienne pushed the numbers, like in spy movies. He's so bad with electronics, he's sure that if he touches it, it'll short out and maybe explode. Nothing catches his attention. Nothing—

"I don't know," he says. "I don't know which one."

Another resounding thud, and the door groans inward, straining on its track.

"Hey." Vivienne catches his hand and squeezes it. Their eyes meet, and he can see the fierce determination behind the hazy violet of the drugs. "Relax. You got this."

The anxiety lessens a little, and he lets out a breath he didn't even realize he was holding. "I don't know," he says. "You pick—"

She pulls his hand down toward the panel, and he twitches his finger aside to press one of the buttons. It's the number eight, in fact. The panel lights up green, and the door swishes open.

"Huh," Vivienne says, visibly relaxing. "Good call, Godsight."

"What?"

"That power, it's called Godsight," she says. "Justice had it, and I guess if you're his kid—"

The door across the way bursts off its track with an explosion of screaming metal and clatters ten feet into the room. A-Girl staggers through, heaving, head down and hair stringy with sweat and dust. She glares at them and tries to say something, but it turns into a cough.

"Time to go." Vivienne grabs his hand and hauls him into the corridor beyond.

They get inside, and she hits the emergency close. Orestes glances back, and A-Girl is hurtling toward them like a fastball, one fist held out before her like a spear. She angles her flight toward the closing gap but doesn't make it in time. There's a muted *whump*, and Orestes and Vivienne both wince. Then her face appears behind the glass, her expression furious, and she smacks her hand on the door.

"Let's go," Vivienne says. "The lab is this way."

22. DO YOU EVEN FIGHT, SIS?

"It's weird that they didn't kill you," Vivienne says as they head down the hall, lights buzzing on as they pass under them. "I mean, good, yay, you're alive, but The Raven programmed their IFF sensors comprehensively. They should have fried you, no problem. Are you good with robots?"

"I don't think so," Orestes says. "I mean, I'm shit at electronics. I can't even use a smartphone."

"What do you mean?" she asks shrewdly. "Like, you're really clumsy and you drop them?"

"Nah," he says. "I mean, just, every phone I've ever used has issues. Malfunctions, shuts off randomly, or the battery life wears out super fast. That's why I have this." He pulls out his flip phone, which is at least eight years old. "As long as I charge it every couple hours, it's ok."

"Hmm." Vivienne brushes her hand against his thigh. "How about now?"

Orestes swallows a nervous lump in his throat, and the lights flicker in the hallway. "The fuck?"

"Thought so." Vivienne takes the hand away. "Performance anxiety. Happened to Justice, too."

"Wait, what—?"

"Here we are."

They reach the end of the hallway, and the sign printed above the door says "Tech Lab." There's also a stylized Raven symbol Orestes recognizes all too well. "You don't mean ... *more* of The Raven."

"Yep. Gotta be something in there we can use." Vivienne punches in a code, and the access panel turns green, then converts to a palm scanner. "Well, I hope he didn't get around to reprogramming this to kill me or anything."

"Does he hate you that much?"

"Oh yeah."

Slowly, she reaches toward the scanner, spreading her fingers wide. Orestes sucks in a breath.

"Ahh!" Vivienne jerks taut when she touches the scanner, her every muscle going tight. Orestes gasps and starts to say something, but then she looks over at him with a wry smile.

"Oh, real mature," he says.

"Relax, kid. Booby traps aren't what The Raven's about. He prefers *active* murder." Light plays over her hand, scanning up and down, and then the panel flashes green.

"Cool. *Cool.* That's cool." Orestes looks back over his shoulder, to where the sounds of A-Girl smashing in the next door have grown much louder. "She's almost through, isn't she?"

"Yep. But don't worry. There's a plan."

"A plan?"

"A plan to have a plan."

As soon as the door slides open, Vivienne pulls Orestes through. He chances to look back and sees an enraged A-Girl flying toward them, costume torn and hair wild. She looks like a pink fireball. The door slides smoothly shut just before she gets there, and there's a loud wham as she crashes into it, yet again. This door isn't as tough as the previous one, so that impact bends it inward a good two inches.

"Um." Orestes looks around, then bites his lip. "I don't see any other exits."

The lab is like something out of a movie, bristling with all sorts of machines and gadgets he doesn't even recognize, let alone know how to use. And he thought the medbay was weird. Of the shelves and shelves of machines, he only recognizes a couple laptops and tablets that look like something he's accustomed to, but colored and constructed totally differently. Most of them are reinforced and protected in thick black cases. He once heard his dad use the word "ruggedized" in reference to a tablet at work, and this fits the descriptor.

Vivienne seems to know what she's looking for, because she checks each of the shelves in turn, scanning them as though looking for a book at a library she hasn't been to in years. "Not the mass accelerator, not the armor piercer—ah, this." Her eyes dawn with recognition, and she runs her hand over something that looks like a heaped bunch of wire. "Yeah, we can use this." As he watches, she unfolds the thing into something that looks a little like a hula-hoop, but thicker. Then she frowns at Orestes. "As long as you stay calm."

"What?" He blinks at her, confused. "What do you mean?"

"Ok," she says. "It's complicated, but here goes. That thing, where you can't use electronics without burning them out? That's electro-agrikinesis. Electric field manipulation." She lays out the hoop of metal just inside the door, totally ignoring the banging sounds. "I'm guessing you can't control it, but when you're excited or scared or something, you short things out. You have anxiety, right?"

"Y-yeah," he says. "I mean—"

"It's fine, we can work with that. But for right now, A-Girl is coming this way, she's too strong for me to fight, and we need this extremely delicate tech to work to stop her. So." Green light flashes from little blinking indicators on the hoop, then goes solid and constant as though ready. Vivienne gestures in what is probably supposed to be a soothing way. "Try to stay calm."

"Um, ok?" Orestes looks back at the door. It has no glass, but he can imagine A-Girl, furious and powerful, on the other side. As he watches, it bends in another inch under a massive blow. "Because that's not scary at all."

At his feet, the circle of metal sparks slightly. The little green lights power up.

"Ok, here we go." Vivienne claps her hands on both sides of Orestes's head and draws his face close to hers. At first, he thinks she's going to kiss him, and shivers run through his body. Seeing her purple eyes that close makes him slightly dizzy. And ...

Nothing.

Well, not *nothing*. There's something there. A hazy weight that settles over him, like growing sleepy all of a sudden, except his body isn't tired. All the fear, the anxiety, even the anticipation of Vivienne's touch—it all just fades away, sucked up as though by a vacuum cleaner. His emotions just drain away, and he's left feeling numb and empty. Dimly, he sees faint purple magic swirling in her eyes, and only when she steps away to the other side of the hoop does he realize what just happened.

She *fed* on him.

"Get behind me," she says, and he does.

Two more hits, and the door screeches open, swinging on its hinges to batter against the wall. There stands A-Girl, pink lightning arcing from her eyes to her hands. Her costume hangs in tatters, exposing long swaths of golden skin and a sensible pink sports bra. She's obviously gone through the wringer, as she's had to fight every single one of The Raven's robots. One of them hangs wrapped around her like a metallic shoulder bag. She seemed really nice back at Devil's Due, but one look at her furious expression this time convinces Orestes to rethink things.

Somehow, he's not afraid, though. He knows how he should be reacting, but the fear just isn't there. Vivienne ripped it all out of him. It feels peaceful, but at the same time, it's like he's outside his own body, watching things without any obvious attachment to any of them. Like this is all a video game that he's watching someone else play.

"Well. Here we are." Vivienne raises her clawed hand and beckons A-Girl forward. "Come on."

The heroine doesn't disappoint. She takes a big step forward, as though to launch herself at them like a missile. Green light flashes up from the hoop, like a reverse waterfall, shrouding her in a curtain of lasers for an instant, and then she lands heavily on her outstretched leg in the middle of the hoop. She staggers and falls to one knee, her furious expression suddenly confused. The pink light is gone, too, and she looks incredibly tired, as though she just ran a marathon.

Casually, Vivienne takes off her claw and hands it to Orestes. "Hold this," she says.

He takes it without comment, surprised at how cold and light it is. Those claws are sharp.

"What?" A-Girl asks, looking at her scuffed gloves. "What was—?"

She's so distracted with whatever happened that she doesn't react when Vivienne steps in and launches a punch at the side of her head. That, or with her invulnerability, she just never bothers to defend herself. Either way, A-Girl hardly seems to notice, at least until the hit lands on her cheek and puts her on the floor like a discarded doll. She sprawls with a groan, then looks back up at Vivienne, one hand to her cheek, forehead drawn up in shock.

"Power drainer." Vivienne shakes out her fist, wincing. "Sorry about the hit, but you—"

A-Girl surges up with a cry and lunges at Vivienne, who casually steps aside and shoves her the other way into a rack of gadgets. Gizmos go clattering to the floor as A-Girl balances against a desk.

"Oh, come on," Vivienne says. "You can't be serious."

With a snarl, A-Girl comes at her again, flailing with wild swings. Without her claw, Vivienne has a lot more options. She slips the first couple punches, then twists aside as A-Girl launches a right-cross right at her face. Vivienne catches her arm under her own and lashes out with her free hand, striking A-Girl on the inside of the elbow, then across the cheek. She naturally falls, and Vivienne locks her arm up, trapping her in a hold. A-Girl half-sits, half-kneels, growling and cursing in frustration and pain.

"Did no one ever teach you to fight?" Vivienne asks. "Now you're just—"

A-Girl head-butts Vivienne right in the gut, which surprises her so much she lets go of the hold. Vivienne winces, grasping herself over the site of her recent surgery, and her eyes flash with fear energy.

Orestes watches the two grapple, one clumsy, the other trying very hard not to hurt her, and wants to intercede. But there's nothing inside him. It all feels so far away ...

Vivienne gets A-Girl's arm behind her back and wrestles her to the floor. "Just—dammit!"

Purple energy flares, and A-Girl's body goes rigid, then slumps to the floor. He thinks she's breathing, but it's hard to tell. The floor looks very inviting. He's had a hard day. He sits down.

"Kid," Vivienne says. "Hey kid, are you all right? Oh crap, did I—?"

A dreamless sleep beckons.

23. GROUPING AND REGROUPING

The first thing Marcus Orestes sees when he wakes up is the sunlight streaming through the window, reflecting off the TV of his off-campus apartment just off Ravenna. It's south facing, so it gets some good sun during the day, if there's any sun to be had that day in Seattle. The sun illuminates a thousand spilling dust motes in the air, and it occurs to him that he should really dust in here soon.

The second thing he sees, when he turns his head just a little to the side, is Vivienne Cain's sleeping face. She's sleeping on her side, one arm under her head, and they're practically eye-to-eye. Her eyeshadow has run a little, giving her raccoon eyes, but in an appealing sort of way. And she's wearing one of his t-shirts. She shifts slightly, murmuring in her sleep. She sounds pleased.

Then and only then does Orestes start freaking out.

He bolts upright on the couch, suddenly breathing heavily, covered in sweat. It's his own living room, and it's burning hot. The thermostat must be at max. At some point, he must have shed his shirt, because he's only got on a pair of blue boxers. At least he and Vivienne are sleeping on two separate couches, arranged around a coffee table covered in pizza boxes, soda cans, and wireless console controllers. And two bottles of hard liquor: one empty Jack Daniels, one half-empty Grey Goose.

Oh God.

She makes a faint sound, and he freezes still. He can't move. Can barely think.

His head feels heavy, and it occurs to him this might be what a hangover feels like. He tries to remember what happened last night, but there's just nothing. Emptiness. He remembers the morning, the funeral, seeing Vivienne Cain (*Lady Vengeance!*), her powers, following her, the fight, the mad drive to SoDo, and then it gets a little weird. Still clear—he can still remember everything that happened right up until they got into the tech room, Vivienne hit A-Girl with the power drainer, and then ...

"Mmf." Vivienne's eyes flutter open, and she plasters one hand over her face. "What time is it?"

"Uh." Orestes looks at the analog clock on the wall, which is built to look like Big Head's big head, with his body and arms indicating the hour, minute, and seconds. It's a collector's item, that clock, at least twelve years old from before Supergroup broke up, but he can't stop the same thought echoing again and again in his head: *oh God, she's going to think I'm such a dork.*

Rightly, as it happens.

"It's 7:43," he says.

She groans. "AM or PM?"

"Uh." He consults the window and the narrow January sunlight. "I think it's morning."

"Fuuuuck," she says, drawing out the word in protest. She rolls over onto her back and grinds the heels of both hands into her eye sockets. Orestes tries very hard not to look at her. "I need a drink."

As if the request finally gives him permission, he springs up like a shot and scrambles to the kitchen. The sink is full of dishes, and he opens the small dishwasher, which is full of what look like clean dishes. He grabs a water glass and heads over to the fridge, where he peers into the cold florescent light. Orange juice, right? That's what you're supposed to drink when you're hungover. Or is it milk? Just water? Man, no beer or anything, it looks like his dads' fridge. Jesus.

He selects the orange juice and shuts the door, revealing the man standing right on the other side of the door. The glass and orange juice both tumble out of Orestes's hands, and while the orange juice lands on the counter and spurts juice all over, the glass bounces off and shatters on the floor. *Shit.*

His roommate is staring at him, big blue eyes wide as plates. He doesn't seem to have noticed the broken glass at all. "Dude!" Chuck says. "Dude. *What.*"

"Shit," Orestes says as he reaches for another glass. "Keep it down. She—"

130

"Hey," Vivienne calls from the other room. "You all right?"

"Yes!" He gives Chuck a panicked look. "Dude, I can explain."

"Dude." Chuck points to his purple T-shirt, which happens to have a faded picture of Lady Vengeance across his broad chest. In one of the really cheesecake nineties outfits that made sense at the time, but these days seems obviously in poor taste. "Are you banging a cosplayer?"

"What? No, I—ow!" Orestes forgot about the glass, and pain sparks up from his foot. He lifts his leg and looks at the piece of glass stuck in the ball of his foot. Dammit. "Look, just—"

"Ok," she says from the other room. "You're not doing anything weird to my drink, are you? Because the last guy who tried to drug me, I carved my initials in his taint."

"Jesus." Chuck grins wide. "That almost sounds like something the real Lady V would say—"

Orestes stares at him, and Chuck blinks.

"No," he says. "Really? That's—" He lowers his voice to a whisper. "That's really her?"

"You don't know?" Orestes asks. "What happened last night?"

"I dunno, Alex had a thing," Chuck said. "You know how it is."

Orestes groans. "Are you guys dating yet?"

"Whaaaat." Chuck tries to look nonchalant as he sweeps up the glass. "You *know* he just broke up with Florian last month ..."

Orestes knows that look, which Chuck always puts on when he's being cagey. "So it's just, what, platonic sleepovers?"

"Oh, sweet boy, the things you don't know," Chuck says. "But stop trying to change the subject. Is that really—" He narrows his eyes and puts on a scowl in a passable imitation of Lady Vengeance from one of her Oprah interviews "—*her?*"

Her voice rises again. "Can I just drink all this liquor by myself? Oh, wow, looks like I can."

"Oh. My god." Chuck puts a hand on Orestes's shoulder. "O, you're my, um—" He does some mental math. "—eighth best friend, and you've always been there for me, so you go get yourself cleaned up, and I'll do this for you. Let me do this."

"Um, do what?" Orestes asks.

"Perfect. Don't worry about a thing."

Chuck scoops up the orange juice, a bottle of sparkling wine from the fridge, and two fresh glasses—champagne glasses,

Orestes notes—and scoots out of the room. "Who wants mimosas!"

"Oh, thank God," Vivienne says. "The gay roommate."

"I'm *such* a fan," Chuck says. "Tell me *everything*."

Jesus, *why*.

Orestes starts to follow him, then winces. The piece of glass pulses in his foot. Dammit. He hobbles past the living room, where Chuck and Vivienne are busy becoming best friends, toward the bathroom. As confusing and surreal as all this is, it could always be worse.

The door swings inward as he reaches for the handle, and standing there, a big gray towel wrapped around the middle third of her body, Angel regards him, his toothbrush hanging out of her mouth. She's fresh from the shower and has a second towel wrapped around her hair like a volleyball attached to her head. Her big eyes are remarkably brown, and he realizes she must wear contacts that make her eyes silvery.

When she's in costume.

As A-Girl.

Angel DeSantes. A-Girl. Daughter of The Raven and Athena. Heir to heroes. In his apartment.

"Oh," she says.

"Um," he says.

They stare at each other for a second, and her face falls slightly, as though remembering something seeing him had made her forget. "I found a new toothbrush in the cupboard," she says, her voice a little irritated. "This isn't yours. Just so you know."

"Oh, uh, good?"

Angel rolls her eyes and slams the door closed.

Because that. *That* makes sense.

"*Jesus*, you have no idea," Vivienne says from the living room, followed by hers and Chuck's combined laughter. Odds are good it was something about Orestes. *Great.*

Orestes has almost forgotten why he's there at the bathroom door but moving his foot sparks fresh pain to job his memory. He knocks softly, then a little more insistently when there's no reply. Angel jerks the door open, and this time she's removed the towel, and her hair hangs loose. He can see the darker roots coming in

132

under the mess of wet blonde curls that hang down to her lower back.

"*What*," she says, not really a question.

"My, uh, foot?" Orestes stands on one foot so he can show her the piece of glass in the wound.

Maybe he expected more sympathy, but she just kind of stares blankly at the wound, then up at him. "And? What do you want me to do about it?"

"Um," he says.

"Jesus," she says. "I mean, first you drain my powers, then you kidnap me, then you run out of hot water, and now, what, I'm supposed to feel sorry for you?" She sounds pissed.

"Kidnapped? Huh?"

She glowers at him.

"Can I get a band-aid or something? They're in the cabinet over the sink, next to the—"

She shuts the door in his face again. There's the sound of rummaging in the cabinet, and the door opens again. She thrusts the box of one-size band-aids at him. "Fabric, huh?" she asks.

"Yeah, my, uh, skin doesn't do well with latex."

"Same," she says. "Which is funny, considering."

"Huh?" Orestes realizes. "Oh, right, the suit. Um—"

She shuts the door in his face.

He's about to turn back toward the living room when the door opens again, and Angel holds up a little orange pill bottle. She's frowning. "What's Propranalol? Are you a junkie, too?"

"Oh, it's a beta blocker, for anxiety," Orestes says. "I have an anxiety disorder."

"Oh," she says, her expression going a little more somber. "Like Xanax?"

"Um."

Another of those awkward little moments passes between them, and she looks a little more sympathetic. Finally, she mumbles something and shuts the door. At least she doesn't slam it.

Only more confused, Orestes limps back down the hall to the living room. There he finds Vivienne and Chuck lounging on the couches, having polished off the champagne and the orange juice, trading stories and jokes like old friends. Like, if he didn't know his roommate was gay, he'd think they were having a morning-after flirt. And it hits him that he's the one who's part of the "morning after," and he has no idea what that entails.

"What you got there, kid?" Vivienne asks.

"Oh my God, your foot," Chuck says, then starts giggling. He's only been legal for a few months, but he's never had much of a tolerance for alcohol. Orestes suspects he had one mimosa, which means Vivienne must have drank the rest of the bottle. Even now, she's working on the vodka.

"C'mere," she says, beckoning. "Lemme see."

Orestes isn't too sure about putting his wounded foot in the hands of a drunk woman, but it's not like he has much of a choice. "I should have got tweezers or something," he says.

"No worries." Vivienne puts his foot up on her bare thigh and inspects the glass sliver. With a tiny frown, she waves her fingers through the air, trailing little purple trails of energy that resolve and shape themselves into what looks like a tiny pair of pliers. Chuck whistles in admiration. Orestes averts his eyes, and not just because Vivienne's purple eyes seem to glow.

"Relax, kid. I got this."

He half-expects her to stab his foot with the fear tweezers, but with surprising steadiness, she extracts the little bloody shard of glass and holds it up to inspect in the daylight. She starts to put it down, but Chuck splutters something to make her pause. He plucks out a tissue and puts it down on the table, and Vivienne drops the tiny bit of glass on the tissue. She waves the tweezers away and returns her attention to Orestes's foot, which she sponges clean with another tissue.

"We should really disinfect that," Chuck says. "Hang on."

He heads down the hall to the bathroom, leaving them alone in the room together. Vivienne raises an eyebrow and pulls out a small tube of antiseptic that was in the first aid box. Orestes watches as she applies the cream to the band-aid, then bandages him up. Those hands beat down A-Girl the previous night, but now they're surprisingly gentle, and Orestes finds it captivating.

"There." Vivienne leans down to inspect her handiwork and looks up at him under a stray lock of her black hair. "Does it hurt?"

"No," Orestes says. "Well, a little."

She smiles, slightly drunkenly. Then, softly, she kisses his foot over the bandage, simultaneously like a mother treating a scraped knee and very, *very* not that. Orestes isn't sure what to say or do. He just stares at her, heart pounding in his head.

"Welp," she says. "Gotta pee."

She shoves his leg unceremoniously away and levers herself off the couch. Without another word, she heads toward the bathroom and slips around Chuck coming the other direction, his eyes wide. She murmurs something soft.

"Dude," Chuck says. "*Dude.*"

At first, Orestes isn't sure what he's talking about, but then he sees Angel and Vivienne face to face in the hallway. Gone is the towel, and now A-Girl has on one of Chuck's old Supergroup XL tee shirts, primarily depicting Justice, which hangs down almost to her knees.

It really doesn't make the situation any better.

24. DOMESTIC DISASTER

"Angel," Vivienne says.

"Aunt V."

Angel crosses her arms, and it's clear she means to say more, but then Vivienne goes into the bathroom and shuts the door. Angel rolls her eyes, sighs, and walks past Orestes out to the little kitchen.

As soon as they're both out of sight, Chuck looks back to Orestes, his face flushed, his eyes sparkling. There might as well be stars there. "Dude, dude, dude, *dude!*"

Orestes puts his hand on Chuck's shoulder. "Um, I'll tell you when I figure it out?"

"*Dude.*"

He leaves Chuck to dissolve into a fanboy puddle there in the hallway and makes his way cautiously back to the kitchen. There he finds Angel struggling with a glass jar of home-canned peaches over the sink, her face red with more than exertion and her dark brows knit in consternation. Beside her on the counter stands a box of one of Chuck's very sugary enriched cereals. She's muttering to herself, and none of it sounds particularly complimentary.

"Um," Orestes says. "Aren't you super strong?"

"Yah!" Startled, Angel whirls around, and the jar practically disintegrates in her hands, exploding into several chunks of slimy glass, syrup, and pink-orange fruit. It sprays all over her shirt, the counter, and the floor. She sucks in a sharp breath. "Jesus! Don't sneak up on people!"

"Sorry," Orestes says with a wince. "Are you ok?"

137

"Do I *look* ok?" Her eyes seem to flare with pink light, which vanishes just as quickly, though the color in her cheeks remains. She glowers. "Jesus, I'm gonna have to take another shower now. *Fuck*."

"I mean did you cut yourself," he says. "You know, on the glass."

"Oh." She blinks, as though the possibility never occurred to her. "No, uh, I don't think so."

"Let me see?" Careful not to cut his foot again, Orestes steps closer, and she holds out her hands for his inspection. Sure enough, they're sticky with peach syrup but intact—they feel really soft, in fact. "I don't get it," he says. "You—"

Then he realizes he's holding her hands, and she's staring at him with points of color high on her cheeks. She's biting her lip. He lets go of her hands and she retracts them after a second of hesitation. They stand there in silence for a second, and Orestes is aware of his heart pounding loud enough that there's no way she can't hear it. She doesn't even have super hearing, does she?

He realizes she's not wearing a bra. *Shit*.

"It's the power drainer." She picks up the broken jar and slops the surviving peaches into a bowl that, miraculously, went untouched by the explosion. There's peaches residue everywhere else, though, including all around the bowl. "Fucks with my powers for a couple days. They come and go."

"So this has happened to you before?"

"Obviously." She flicks a chunk of glass out of the bowl and grabs a spoon from the drying rack.

"Hang on." Orestes grabs the bowl before she can. "You're not gonna eat these, are you?"

"Why not?" she asks. "Invulnerability is in my power set. I can digest glass."

"You just said your powers were in flux."

"Oh. *Right*." Now she looks dubiously down at the peaches, then looks a little ill. "Um."

"It's cool." Orestes opens up the pantry, in which at least six more jars are stacked. "My dads love canning."

She brightens a little. "Oh, thank God."

As she pours the peaches from a new jar—which he opened for her with the aid of some warm water—Orestes shovels the remains of the glass-polluted peaches into the trash and, for the second time this morning, grabs the broom. They have to scoot around each other between the sink and the counter, and they both pick the same way a couple of times, and Orestes tries to defuse the awkwardness with a chuckle. Angel blinks at him, flushes a little, and refocuses on what she's doing: pouring all the peaches into a big mixing bowl and burying them in the rest of the cereal in the box. He has to stare as she taps gingerly at the side of the inverted box, and her hand abruptly goes through it and out the other side in a puff of sugar-saturated enriched wheat dust.

This girl, he realizes, is a little clumsy.

"Oops." She looks at him sheepishly, then extends her hand so he can pull the cereal box off it.

"That," he says, "must be real annoying."

"Tell me about it." Gingerly, she picks up the bowl and goes to town on the peaches and cereal. "Sorry about the grumps. I'm low blood sugar. I've gotta eat like twelve thousand calories a day."

"Jesus." Orestes whistles. "Just, like, *all* the pizza?"

"Pizzas, peanut butter, avocados, milkshakes, ice cream. Like a *lot* of bread."

He grins. "That must be rough."

"I mean, it *sounds* nice," she says with her mouth full. "But you get tired of everything." She lowers the bowl for a second, a feverish hunger in her eye. "What?"

She's got cereal stuck to her chin, which strikes him as adorably funny, but Orestes just shakes his head. He grabs a sponge, but maybe he should wait until she finishes in the kitchen before he cleans up. "You need something else?"

"This should do it—for the morning, at least." She brushes the worst of the peach residue off Chuck's tee shirt. "I'll pay you back. For the shirt, too."

"It's fine. It's just laundry."

She steps in his way and looks him right in the eye, which means she looks up a little. He didn't realize it before, but he's got four, maybe five inches on her. Man, she's *real* close. Like almost touching.

"No," she says, very seriously. "I'll pay you back. It's important."

There's something in the firmness of her gaze that brooks no argument. Until yesterday, Orestes had never met a celebrity or a superhero, much less both, but she doesn't seem like a spoiled rich girl. There's determination there that he recognizes. That, he's seen before.

He swallows. "Ok, sure."

Abruptly, the oven starts randomly beeping, breaking the moment, and he scrambles around to turn off the timer. Nothing on the burner, and the oven isn't on. Just one of those weird electrical disturbances around him. What did Vivienne say? Electro-agrikinesis. Manipulation of electrical fields. A power Justice had ...

Out in the living room, Orestes's roommate and their other guest laugh uproariously. They must have gone back to telling each other salacious stories. It's like they were programmed for each other.

"No kidding," Vivienne says. "This guy I know—superhero— he has a kid named Chuck."

"Yeah? I'd love to meet him!"

"*Her*," Vivienne says. "Girl Chuck."

"That's cool too!" Chuck's voice turns sly. "This *guy you know*?"

She responds with a husky chuckle. "Well—"

The distinctive sounds of Chuck's favorite fighting game drown out whatever she says next.

Orestes isn't sure what to do when Angel's muttering distracts him, and he looks back to see storm clouds sweeping across her face. That pink gleam is back in her eye, and the way she's holding the empty mixing bowl, he expects it to shatter any second.

"Hey," he says. "Can I—?"

He reaches for the bowl, and that breaks her concentration a little. She sighs and hands it over. Their hands touch, and he could swear there's a little spark that passes between them. Her startled expression says she felt it too. Her lips part slightly, like she's going to say something.

Then she's gone. It takes him a second before he's even aware that she left, but when he hears the angry voices, it jars him out of his rapture, and he heads into the living room. He arrives in time to see Angel storm away down the hall and slam his bedroom door.

Vivienne sighs, looking thoroughly disgusted. Another argument. Chuck looks extremely interested in the window all of a sudden.

"What was that?" he asks.

"Family stuff." Vivienne's fully dressed after the bathroom, dressed in her jeans and boots again, and wearing a purple shirt—his shirt, he realizes, which has her stylized V symbol on it. It looks much better on her than it ever did on him. "*Welp*, I'm off. Take care of her, ok?"

"What?" Orestes says.

"Angel." Vivienne pulls on her leather jacket, which still smells faintly of all that blood she got on it. "I told her not to go anywhere until her powers recover. It's a twenty-four-hour drain, tops, so it should be this afternoon. Then have her call her agent or whatever. Not my problem."

"Wait a minute—"

She sidles up to him, and words and thoughts both desert him. She's got a kind of smile that the comics don't really do justice: wry, amused, and just the slightest bit suggestive.

The TV abruptly goes to static, and Chuck moans. "Come on, bruh!"

"Be good." Vivienne plants a kiss on Orestes's cheek. "Thanks for the shirt."

Then she's gone, leaving the lingering scent he's come to associate with her. A heady mix of blood and sweat and booze. The door closes behind her.

"Dude." Chuck is staring at him. "Lady Vengeance *kissed* you."

Orestes blinks.

"*What.*"

25. PAST SINS

"Fuck, fuck, *fuck*," Vivienne repeats to herself as she waits for the elevator.

Nothing happened when she clicked the button the first time, and so preoccupied is she with the string of self-directed invective that it has taken a full minute of nothing happening before she realizes the elevator isn't coming. Only now does she notice the "out of order" sign, which, in retrospect, she realizes she made a note of last night. It took her a minute then, too.

"Fuuuuuuuuck," she says, drawing the word out, and starts toward the stairs. She's wobbly, partly the buzz from the champagne and vodka, partly the influx of existential dread.

That kid is like what, nineteen? Less than half her age. But that's not even the worst of it.

What the fuck is she even doing?

All those years hiding, and even faking her death a couple times. Everything was going fine. And then some kid comes into her bar and all hell breaks loose. Some kind of fucking luck.

And now The Raven is on to her.

Probably.

Definitely.

Shit.

Maybe it's where she is. The kid's apartment building feels like most modern complexes do: a shallow mix of mostly anxiety with occasional seasonings of other, more vibrant emotions. Emotions soak into places over time, and sometimes she can pick up on them, particularly in really old buildings. Which is rarely a good thing. The apartment across the hall gives her a hot spike of anger, just before two women start screaming at each other. It's not just them, but something farther back in the building's past. The deep, *deep* well of despair from the corner apartment at the end of the hall tells her something real bad went down there, but it has faded with time. Suicide, maybe a couple years old. The last thing she needs is to encounter the echoes from something like *that* first thing in the morning.

A door unlatches, and she sees some dude in a hoodie down the hall. Without even thinking about it, she ducks around a corner into a short little hallway with a couple rooms and a window at the end. She watches his dull reflection in the brass lining the elevator, but he doesn't seem to have noticed her. He starts heading the other way toward—there, the glowing green Exit sign. He doesn't seem to be looking for her. Evasion unnecessary.

"Get a hold of yourself, V," she says. "You're shaking like a schoolgirl."

With good reason. Most of the people who live in this building—almost dead center of Capitol Hill, just off Broadway—are probably in the twenty to thirty range, many of them students. She can tell by the buzz of nervous energy—people that age constantly worry about something, be it schoolwork, actual work, debt, romance, sex, whatever—and that's what she absorbs. After burning so much power last night, Vivienne Cain is like a dry sponge, and she soaks up whatever emotional energy she wades through. The drinking can't block that, and by the time she finds the stairs, she's veritably shaking from the anxiety high. The stuff here feels light, tinny, and easily burnt up, like a sugary cola—instant energy, but no depth to it. Not like real, genuine fear, which settles in like a good scotch and burns doing down. She'd *love* some of that.

The two women are shouting so loudly she can hear them all the way down the hall.

She takes a hit from the bottle she palmed from the kid's adorable roommate—boy Chuck—and heads toward the exit. As she passes Orestes's door, it occurs to her to wonder how much of her mood has to do with all the anxiety she's absorbing as opposed to how much is just her own shame.

"Stop hitting on the cute college boy," she says under her breath as she opens the door to the stairwell. "He's just a kid."

Why shouldn't you have what you want?

The voice comes out of nowhere so smoothly, so logical and in sync with the world around her, that Vivienne reacts only belatedly. She blinks, freezes in place, and throws herself back against the wall inside the stairwell and tries not to move. The landing creaks under her weight, and the thinly carpeted stairs seem to yawn below her and above.

Heart thudding in her throat, she looks first up, then down, then back into the hall. Someone has just exited a door at the other end of the hall, but they're way too far away to be that voice.

Did she really hear that? Or did she imagine it?

What do you think, my love?

"No," she says. "Go away."

Vivienne. Really. You should know better.

She sucks in a breath to scream. "Go *fuck* your—"

A stifled cry from just inside the hallway makes her look back, and a young woman—she can't be older than nineteen or twenty, hair cut short, pixie-goth type, shoulder bag, glowing phone in her hand—pulls up short and gives her a look that's half-perplexed, half-judgmental. By the time the look goes from Vivienne's disheveled hair to her unmade-up face to the bottle of vodka in her left hand she didn't even bother to hide behind her leg, it has settled firmly on disgust. Vivienne tries to give her some sort of smile, which probably looks more like a corpse's grimace, and the girl gives her a nice wide berth on her way down the stairs. Wariness and contempt waft off her, and she's probably going to report a strange woman in the stairwell.

Of course, she thinks Vivienne's a crazy wino, and to be fair, it's not like she's wrong.

We could follow her, the voice says. *Shove her when she's not looking. Break her neck.*

She knows that voice.

Vivienne realizes her hands are shaking, and the stairs feel suddenly freezing cold. It's dimly lit and there aren't any windows. It feels a little industrial that way, anonymous and threatening. Great. For one terrible heartbeat, she thinks she sees someone standing in the corner on the next landing, where the stairs turn left. Then the image fades back into the shadows, leaving a lingering image of a dozen eyes: eyes that are mouths full of mismatched snaggle teeth. Grinning at her.

The bottle of vodka comes up and she desperately twists off the cap. It falls from her trembling hands and bounces down the stairs, unheeded. She starts drinking, guzzling the vodka like cool water on a hot day. Her throat works and vodka streams down over her chin and her neck. There was half a bottle left, and she downs it within a minute or so. It burns, but it's a familiar fire, and the last time she gagged on liquor was twenty years ago. By the end of it, she's sunk to the floor, sitting back against the wall, and she shuts her eyes tight against the image.

"Go away," she says. "Go. *Away.*"

Already she can feel it dulling her senses. Her absorption. Her perception.

Dammit. He's found her again.

Fuck.

~

The phone rings in the outer office, which Wren makes some effort to ignore. It never fails: the office can get no calls all day, but the second there's an interesting article in *Psychology Today* ...

The phone rings again, with no sign of anyone picking it up.

"Mary?" Wren calls out, but of course there's no response. The clock says 1:04, and since Mary started dating that skater boy, she consistently gets back from lunch at least ten minutes late. Wren gives that relationship two months.

The office is set up for clinical comfort: a couch perfectly balanced between soft and firm, wall art of flowers and natural landscapes, a trickling fountain in the corner. The fan unit, necessary even in winter in Chicago thanks to an aging building with over-active radiator heat, kicks in and sends a wave of soothing cool air. That's the word: soothing. Comfortable. Every piece of the room's décor is intended to do that for clients, to encourage them to relax and open up. It works on everyone who comes in here, except for Wren themself. There's just something missing.

The phone rings a third time and, with a sigh, Wren picks it up. "This is Dr. Fulton."

There's a pause—a breathy silence—and the person on the other end fumbles the phone a little. Wren's about to hang up when she finally speaks, in a voice they never expected to hear again.

"Hey, Birdie."

"Who—" Wren sits up straight, startled. "Who is this?"

"It's me, Wren."

"Jesus." Wren can barely whisper. "*V.*"

"Yeah."

It *is* her, plus half a lifetime of drinking and probably smoking, but she's unmistakable.

Wren is about to scream into the phone, but the door in the outer office creaks open, and Mary's distinctive giggle makes them think better of it. With their enhanced hearing, Wren can make out the two voices, but the phone call is too distracting to focus on the words.

"I—" Wren covers their mouth with their hand, restraining an outburst that wells up in their chest. They cradle the phone against their shoulder and tap on the keyboard to call up a search. It shows a bunch of ten-year-old articles about the destruction of Supergroup Tower, along with a couple links to conspiracy pieces about how Vivienne was supposed to have survived. "I thought you were dead."

On the other end of the line, Vivienne stifles a bitter little laugh. "Not for want of trying," she says. "Sorry about Tony's eye, by the way. I know you two had a thing back in the day."

"Fu—" Wren shakes their head. "Yeah, not after he murdered you."

"Oh. Shit. That tracks."

"V—" Wren rubs their forehead with their free hand. "Are you ok?"

"Was I ever ok?"

"*V.*"

"Just peachy." Vivienne sounds petulant-drunk, which tracks. "Listen, I need—"

Wren can't hold back anymore. "You can't just call me after fifteen fucking years—during which I thought you were dead, by the way—and ask for a favor."

It comes out much louder and sharper than Wren intended, and Mary and her hipster boyfriend suddenly stop talking in the outer room. Great.

Vivienne doesn't speak for a second. Then: "I just wanted to talk, Wren, but if that's not going to happen, I'll—" She laughs bitterly. "You know what? Never mind. This was a fucking terrible idea."

Wren hits mute on the phone, slams the receiver down on the desk, and puts their head in their hands. They breathe heavily, every exhale almost a scream.

The psychology degree kicks in hard, pushing to start a dialogue and soothe someone in need, but at the same time, Wren feels a rising wave of emotion they thought long ago dealt with. Grief, frustration, anger—a *lot* of anger. And love, too. There was a time, twenty years ago, when Wren loved this woman very, very deeply, and they realize only now that those feelings didn't just go away. All those psych classes, grad school, and almost two decades of helping people through things like this, and they never really understood that. Until right now.

There's a gentle knock on the door. "Dr. Fulton?" Mary asks. "Is everything all right?"

"Yes. Thanks, Mary."

The light flashes. The line is still open. Vivienne is still breathing on the other end. Whatever words she conjures up, Wren hears more in that pause than any objection or expletive.

"Well," Vivienne says. "I guess—"

Wren unmutes the line and brings the phone to their ear. "Wait."

"Yeah?" Vivienne's voice sounds weak. Hopeful, maybe.

Wren wets their lips, thinking of how to handle this. When they were kids, Wren eventually worked out how to talk to Vivienne, but so much time has passed, would the same strategies work? Wren needs to know what's wrong—needs to fix it, or at least make sure Vivienne could handle it. And if she's calling, out of the blue, after fifteen years, it's something she needs help to handle.

"Vivienne," Wren says.

"What?"

Wren takes a deep breath. *V, I love you*, they could say, or *V, we'll get through it together*, or maybe just *V, it's ok*. None of those, though. Wren just speaks the truth in their heart.

"Vivienne, you deserve to be happy."

Silence.

"Yeah, well, what the fuck do you know?"

The call ends, leaving Wren staring down at the phone clutched in their hand. They blink.

Wren reaches one trembling finger over to the phone and presses the intercom button. "Mary?" they ask. "Cancel my appointments for this afternoon."

"Dr. Fulton? But—"

"And take the rest of the day off."

Wren switches off the intercom, hand shaking more than before. They sit, forcibly calm, until Mary and her boyfriend are long out of the office.

Then, with a scream from deep in their core, Wren picks up the monitor and hurls it shattering against the wall. Glass and plastic rain across the office, but Wren isn't done. Crouched, they flip the desk over with another scream, then smash the soothing, low-watt lamp against the bookshelf full of psych books. The bookshelf goes over next, spilling its contents all over. Wren grabs the mountain waterfall art off the wall, bends it in half, and smashes that into the floor as well. Then they get to the couch—the stupid, fucking, uncomfortable couch—and flip it over with a surge of corded muscle.

There, beneath where the couch had sat, there's a briefcase, and only the sight of it brings Wren's rampage to a halt. They gaze down, from the wreck of the office, and slowly kneel. With trembling fingers, Wren puts in the combination they haven't used in years but remember by heart.

The lid pops open, revealing the contents of the case: a black and white mask on top of an impeccably folded, skin-tight suit of the same color scheme.

Wren scowls. "Dammit, Vivienne Cain."

~

Vivienne Cain crouches in the stairwell for a time, huddled against the wall as though hiding from something only she could see. Her behavior has been erratic, resembling that of a druggie either climbing up to a really powerful high or coming down from one. But it's definitely her, and when she finally leaves, the distinctive scent of her hair and her body linger in the space.

Definitely her.

He lurks, hidden unseen in the darkened corner of the stairwell near the high ceiling, until at least two minutes after he's certain she has left the building. Then he scuttles down to where she stood and bends low to smell her. He presses his nose to the carpet where she sat, inhaling the particular fragrance of her juices. He wants so badly to taste them.

With a quick glance to make sure no one is watching, he slips out a long, orange tongue and touches it to the floor. Runs his tongue along the gritty carpet. *Tastes her.*

Every muscle shivers in pleasure. At last. He's waited so long ...

Voices. His body tenses, alert to a potential threat, and his eyes roll up to look up the stairs toward the third floor. Movement. Shadows lengthen and flow. Someone coming.

He skitters down the stairs, over the rail and around. He huddles in the darkened corner of the stairwell and licks at his fingers. Yes. She will be his.

But how?

26. BREAKING STUFF

———

Of all the mornings in recent memory, Orestes can say, with confidence, that this one is definitely the weirdest. Through the door to his room, he can hear agitated shout-whispering and the occasional crunch of wood or snapping plastic, punctuated by some very creative profanity. Considering how much of his stuff Angel seems committed to breaking, it's probably a good thing Orestes accepted her insistence on paying him back.

At least it's Friday, and he has no classes on Friday. He doesn't even work tonight.

He senses a presence looming in the hallway behind him and looks back to see Chuck lurking over his shoulder, his face enraptured. "What," Orestes says.

"Dude," Chuck says. "And you have powers? Why didn't you tell me, bruh?"

"Because A, please don't call me that, and B, yesterday was the first I'd heard of it."

"It makes a lot of sense, though," Chuck says. "Uncontrolled electro-agrikinesis causes all kinds of problems. Explains why you can't use phones, why your computers break down after a month or two, things like that. Like, in his self-titled run, number 7, Nerve the Conductor shorted out an entire computer lab at his school just because he got an email about his uncle dying—"

Chuck's encyclopedic knowledge of superheroes and comic books has always staggered Orestes, who knows a lot about comics but is, by comparison, a total newbie. He was super into them when he was a kid, but these days he reads comics merely for—gasp—fun. He is what Chuck affectionately describes as a "cute but *filthy* casual."

"Wait, how'd you know about my—" He winces. "V told you."

Chuck's eyes go wide. "She slept with you, she kissed you, and you call her 'V'?" he says. "You sure you two aren't together? Little nicknames are basically printed on your ticket to bone-town."

"Jesus," Orestes says, looking for an escape route. Typically, when Chuck badgers him like this, he shuts himself in his room and puts on music to drown him out. But Angel's in there. He feels oddly homeless. "Don't you have morning classes?"

"Sociology, but there's so much to observe right here." Chuck grins wider. "Like, are you going after both of them? You know they're related, right? That's a little weird—"

Orestes closes the bathroom door on Chuck and stands there looking at himself in the mirror until his roommate finally gives up and leaves. He's shaking, and little blue sparks glide out of him toward Chuck's electric toothbrush and shaver, which are both plugged in to charge. It's funny, he's never actually seen electricity come out of himself like this, but it's so obvious he wonders why he didn't see it before. The shaver goes nuts and burns out, and the toothbrush charger whines until the green light turns red, then blinks out entirely. The sparks start making their way along the cords ...

"Shit."

Lest he blow out the entire circuit for the building, Orestes unplugs both appliances, then ducks out of the bathroom and into the hallway with its safe lack of electronics. Chuck gave up, which is a relief, but the way he's smiling at him from the living room says there's going to be more later. Great.

Orestes stands there in the cool darkness, practicing breathing techniques to calm himself. Come to think of it, with all the crazy of this morning, he didn't take his meds. He should probably ...

Behind the door to his room, there's an electronic whine and a disconsolate sound of something powering off, and Orestes can distinctly hear Angel say "welp."

Before he can think about it, Orestes finds himself knocking on the door.

There's a pause.

"Um, come in?"

Orestes, who wasn't even aware of knocking, is suddenly gripped by the terrible realization that he did. And now he has two options: go in, or make some sort of excuse to stay out. Which situation would be more awkward?

Too late. He's already pushing through the door.

His room is a mess, and it's not entirely his fault. Some of the mess is standard for a busy college student who doesn't have time to clean: the bedsheets tangled, clothes spilling out of the closet, papers strewn all over his desk and around, that sort of thing. But some of it is new: the broken CRT with the built-in VHS player, for instance. Not new because the appliance is new, but because it didn't use to have Angel's arm extended from it. There she stands, half-bent over next to the desk, one hand on the back of the desk chair for balance, trying to pull her hand out of the punctured screen. She looks at him sheepishly with the kind of embarrassed expression one might expect from someone caught changing. The unexpected intimacy of the moment steals away whatever words he was prepping when he opened the door.

"Hey, uh, sorry about your TV?" She lifts her arm, picking the hapless thing up like a five-pound weight. "This *is* a TV, right?"

"It's an old CRT from the nineties," he says. "My dad had it when he was in college."

"Oh. Um." She pulls her undamaged arm out of the television box. "I tripped."

"It's fine," Orestes says, relieved. "It doesn't really work anyway. Half the time I turn it on, it's just static."

She furrows her brow. "Like, because of your powers, you mean?"

"That or it's really old." Orestes sighs. "Does everyone know more about my powers than I do?"

"I mean, maybe. I heard Aunt V talking about it." Her expression turns stormy, and she looks away. Orestes sees a smartphone in her hand.

"Is that Chuck's phone?" he asks. "Did you, um—?"

"Steal it?" A-Girl gives him a mischievous little smile. "I mean, I borrowed it. Wanted to know where I was and stuff." The phone lights up and, as if on cue, the harsh apartment buzzer goes off to indicate someone at the door. "And I ordered pizza, obviously."

Five minutes later, two heavy, stuffed, deep-dish style pies from the Boston-style pizza place up in U-Village are stacked on his desk—one spinach, one the "mighty meaty"—while Angel sits cross-legged on his bed, distractedly munching away and surfing the web on the phone. She doesn't want to go out into the apartment, and Orestes is fine with having her in his room. It's not the first time a girl's been in here, and she seems, well, *normal.* That helps him keep the electric anxiety under control, so as not to short out Chuck's phone. That, and sitting in the corner as far from her as possible, once he brings them tea.

"So," he says eventually. "Uh, A-Girl?"

"Hrm." She pauses between bites on her second piece of pizza. "Marcus. I slept in your bed. I'm wearing your roommate's shirt. I've gone number two in your bathroom. You can call me Angel."

"Oh." His face feels warm. "Ok."

She devours the slice of what looks more like a cheese casserole than pizza, then takes her time picking out another. She waves for him to ask his question.

"What exactly happened last night?" Orestes asks. "I don't really remember."

"Oh." She puts the latest slice back down and her expression gets cloudy, undermined somewhat thanks to a bit of marinara sauce on her chin. "Aunt V fed on you, beat the shit out of me, then carried us both out to that convertible you were driving. I think she ditched it somewhere down by SafeCo and took an Uber here."

"Wait. An *Uber?*" Orestes can't help but smile at how silly it all is. "Superheroes take Uber?"

"Well, you probably wouldn't want a stolen car parked out in front of your apartment." Angel shrugs. "I mean, I assume it was stolen. That's kind of her MO."

"That, and Friday night parking is just crap anywhere near Broadway."

"Yeah, I was just gonna ask about the Cap Hill apartment thing." Angel picks up the mug of tea from the table, which has mostly cooled off by now. "I didn't want to assume. Like, you don't *seem* gay."

"Oh." Orestes smiles awkwardly. "That's Chuck. I'm straight. Er, mostly."

"Mostly?" Angel quirks up one dark eyebrow.

"Well, I mean, if Jaccob Stevens came to my door right now. Or Marcus Castile—"

"Oh—" Angel nods. "Story checks out. You're a capechaser."

Orestes spews the tea. "What," he says, spluttering. "That's—that's not what I—"

Angel smiles wide. "Ha! Your face! Like, oh-em-gee!" Chuck's phone clicks, and Orestes realizes she took a picture. "I gotta send this to Friday."

"Friend of yours?"

"My *chica buenita* back east." Her face falls. "Aw, man! I don't remember her number. I'll check the JOS fanpage on Twitter. I'm sure Yumi likes it at least." She clicks on the phone, no doubt adding her own account to Chuck's app.

Orestes's eyes widen at the mention of the name Yumi. Surely, it can't be the same one. But he also doesn't want to ask. Instead, he focuses on the part he doesn't understand. "Joss?" Orestes is pretty sure that wasn't actual Spanish. "Like the director, you mean?"

"Jay-oh-ess. Justice or Something, they're, like, teen superheroes. Out of Cobalt City. You know, Johnny Turbo, Dulcamara, Dr. Harada, The Electric Girl, Mara—Murray—uh, Ninja Girl?" Angel grins. "Jeez. What kind of capechaser are you?"

"I'm not."

Orestes thinks about all those nights "reading" Supergroup comics, particularly the Vengeance Vamp run between issues 87 and 94, when Lady V was temporarily turned into a vampire—not that you could really tell. When he was fifteen, he had a poster of Lady V in the classic V-neck/V-area costume up on his wall. To this day, he still deletes his search history regularly.

Ok, so maybe she's not entirely wrong.

"Oh, here it is: NinjaGirlWant2<3. Obviously that's Yumi." Angel clicks away and types a rapid message. "Don't you go to U-Dub, though?"

Orestes is halfway through a sigh of relief, pretty sure the Yumi he knows wouldn't be caught dead with a screenname like that. But then he realizes Angel has asked him a question. "What?"

"You've got an apartment in Cap Hill, and you don't fly," she says. "Seems like a commute."

"Oh. I just, uh, take light rail. See?" He moves over closer to her and points out the window, just over her shoulder. "You can see the station from ... here—"

Only then does he realize exactly how close they are, as she looks up at him with really big hazel-brown eyes. He has to lean over the bed to get to the window, and it puts their faces almost on the same level. He can taste her breath, as she's breathing shallowly right into his nose. The peppermint tea has overwhelmed the pizza, and her breath smells really nice.

"Uh," he says. "Yeah, it's just a couple blocks."

"Oh," she says. "That's ... that's cool."

What is he doing? He's way up in her personal space, and she's on his bed, and ... But she hasn't pulled away. She just sits there, breathing, looking up at his face, her cheeks a little flushed, her expression hesitant. She wets her lips with her tongue but doesn't say anything.

Does ... does she want him to kiss her? Does he want to?

Yes, yes, he does. He definitely wants to kiss her.

But he doesn't.

Mostly because she didn't ask.

And it'd be weird for him to ask. Wouldn't it? It would.

And partly because someone knocks on the apartment door, interrupting their moment. Electricity zaps out and hits Chuck's phone, making it blink twice, then shut down.

"Sorry." Orestes winces and draws away.

"No, it's—" Angel shakes herself. "I kinda have a boyfriend."

"Oh." Orestes tries not to feel crushed. "Wait, kinda?"

"You know, uh, Tom Pierce? Blue Steel?"

Orestes blinks. "You're dating Blue Steel?"

"Tom and I, well, we're sort of dating." She seems embarrassed. "Celebrity dating."

"Celebrity—isn't he like forty?"

"He's thirty-four." Angel's cheeks turn red, and she closes her eyes. "Look, it was my agent's idea. We mostly just pose for things. Photo shoots and stuff. He's in my next video."

"Video?" The knock comes again, a little more insistently. "Sorry, that's probably Florian, or maybe Randy, coming to check if Chuck is around. Randy knows the code, but he doesn't have an actual key. They're at the code-not-key stage of their relationship. Uh, I'll be right back."

"Yeah, ok." Angel looks out the window.

156

At the door, Orestes clears his throat, about to say something, but he thinks better of it. He heads out to the living room. Really, things should be fine, but he can't stop thinking that he blew it.

Blue sparks dance around his fidgeting hands.

~

Angel sighs, looking out the window at the overcast day.

"Jesus, Angel," she says under her breath. "You really blew it."

To be fair, she's had a weird twenty-four hours. She got involved in not one, not two, but *three* significant fist fights, the last of which ended with her kidnapped by her not-actually-dead aunt and waking up in some strange dude's bed. Granted, the dude in question wasn't there at the time, and he seems pretty decent, but still. And she missed her afternoon photo test. Parker's probably going nuts right about now, texting her phone and pinging her helmet, both of which she lost *somewhere* in industrial Seattle.

Goddamn Aunt V.

Angel should have known. Ten years—ten years she's thought her aunt was dead, but really she was just in hiding, and ... Goddammit. Not only should she have known, she shouldn't have been surprised. And really, was she? She's pretty proud of how well she's taken all of this, honestly. Just another day in her increasingly weird life.

She was pretty young when Supergroup perished, but she remembered being not scared, not sad, but really angry. Angry that they would go and get themselves killed and leave her all alone. She didn't remember how she got out of the building, but the news said she was the only survivor. Well, her and The Raven, but she didn't find out about that until later. So was it really such a big surprise that someone else might have made it out alive?

She should really call Parker, but on the one hand, she doesn't remember his number, and on the other, she doesn't really feel like listening to his freak-out. Particularly when he asks where she is, and she tells him she crashed in some random dude's bed. A really *cute* random dude, but still.

Sometimes, she worries about Parker's heart.

Idly, Angel polishes off the last of the two pizzas, down to the last piece. Since the year she spent with the Rogers, where they only fed her a thousand calories a day—about a tenth of what her powers consume every day—she's perfected the skill of eating without really thinking about it. There's just one last piece of spinach deep-dish, which has mostly cooled down. Should she go microwave it? Probably.

When she gets to the door, it occurs to Angel that Marcus should be back by now. He just went to check the door, after all. Did he have to leave to get to class or something? According to Chuck's phone before it died, it's Friday, so maybe he has classes, but Marcus didn't say anything about classes. Did she freak him out or something? The guy seems pretty high-strung. She almost calls out to him, but that feels silly. She should just go find him.

When she heads out into the hallway, there's a surprising amount of noise. It sounds like Chuck turned on the TV and cranked up the volume to max, and it makes the ache that's been looming in Angel's head redouble. The power drainer yesterday already messed with her high strength and low coordination, and now she feels even clumsier.

"Hey," she calls. "Can you turn it down?"

No response, and the volume remains at max.

Hand on her forehead, Angel heads out toward the living room, expecting to find Chuck on the couch, and maybe Marcus doing something, but no one's there. The blanket Chuck was using is still on the couch, rumpled and clearly abandoned carelessly. Did he have to run out of the apartment fast or something? The TV's cranked up to max, and Angel fumbles with the remote, looking for the volume control. She scrolls down from one hundred to eighty or so before she just hits mute. The silence is a relief.

"Chuck?" she asks. "Marcus?"

No response.

She plops down on the couch and clicks through the channels for a bit. There's a guide button, so she presses it, but there's nothing obviously good on. She's starting to get hungry again.

"Hey, you guys?" she asks. "Did you just ditch me or something? Ugh. *Rude.*"

She reaches out with the remote, but something wet drips onto her thumb, and she drops the remote in her surprise. Maybe the ceiling is leaking?

"Ick."

She wipes whatever it was off her hand and sees that her skin has turned a little red with irritation. The remote sits on the coffee table, little plumes of smoke rising from the button pad. It smells faintly of burning.

"What?"

She looks close at the remote, and sees some kind of gunk on it, which makes a faint hissing sound. As she watches, a big green droplet of something lands on the remote, which starts smoldering.

"What the f—?"

Angel looks up and catches her breath.

A form is splayed out against the ceiling, attached with some kind of yellow-green goo, as though someone poured a bunch of glue onto an action figure. Only it's the size of a person, and it takes Angel a second before she recognizes it as Marcus. His big eyes stare down at her, wide and terrified.

She doesn't have the time to ask another question before something moves on the ceiling—a huddled brownish form she initially took for part of the mass of sticky gunk. It's a pot-bellied human form, spindly and bloated at the middle, and it turns its face to her, revealing a too-wide mouth drooling green spittle.

Angel starts screaming.

27. BUSINESS AS USUAL

The bell on the bar door fails to jingle, and Vivienne pauses long enough to try the door again. She closes it, takes a breath, and pulls it open again. No jingle. Two more tries, and she finally realizes the bell fell off and is lying on the floor just inside the boarded-over door. All the windows are boarded over too, and there's still glass on the sidewalk outside.

Figures.

Vivienne pulls the door open a fifth time and strolls in, glass and pieces of wood crunching under her black boots. The place is a goddamn mess, without a single intact table or chair left standing. Almost all the decoration has come down off the walls, there's long, deep sword cuts in the bar, and of course all the windows. It looks condemned, but honestly, it could be worse. *Has* been worse.

"We're closed," sings out a light but tired voice. Andre pauses from where he's sweeping glass and debris from the bar area and looks over at her. "V?"

"Hey," she says. "Anything to drink—?"

He's on her in six big strides, glass crunching under his classy leather loafers, and sweeps her up in his big arms. Vivienne, expecting neither the hug nor the pressure, neglected to take a breath and the room starts spinning, and not just from the vodka. "Get off me," she manages to croak. "Put me down."

He does so, but he's still beaming. "I am so glad you're ok, I'm impervious to the grumps today." He holds her at arm's length for an inspection. "You look terrible, girlfriend."

"Fuck off."

"Ping!" Andre pokes himself in the chest and skips his finger off, which he then holds in the air between them. "See? Impervious!"

"Fuck—" Vivienne looks past him to the bar, where most of the bottles are broken or removed. "Don't tell me we're out of scotch."

It only lasts for a split-second, but she definitely sees Andre's judgmental look. She returns a look that conveys "let's have that fight tomorrow," and he nods at length and heads behind the bar.

He doesn't approve of her drinking, she knows, but he rarely says anything, and then only when she's dared him to do it. That's why she keeps employing him—that, and if she lost him, the business would go under the next day. He takes care of her, she knows that, and sometimes she thinks about how hard it must be for him to see her like this. Fuck, she needs a drink.

Andre takes out one of the few surviving glasses and a dusty bottle. "You wanna tell me what happened last night?" he asks as he pours—on the rocks. "Supervillain?"

"More like a mediocre villain." She takes the glass, downs the contents, and sets it back on the counter. "Aggressively mediocre."

Andre pours again—a double—and she just sips it, then presses the cold glass to her forehead. At least the ice machine is working.

"Punch Man?" he asks. "The Bruiser? The Fister?"

"I *wish* it was the Fister," Vivienne says. "The Pugilist. Small-time muscle for hire. Ugh." She makes a face. "I feel gross just knowing that." She takes another drink.

"Silly question, but—" Andre's lip turns up at the end. "Is he, um, your nemesis?"

Vivienne snorts.

"Ex?" Andre is smiling broadly now.

"Now you're just being hurtful."

"Yeah, you look really hurt." Vivienne's side twinges and she sucks in a breath, making Andre's face fall. "You *are* hurt."

"I'm fine." Vivienne finishes the scotch. "I'm recovering from surgery. Internal bleeding. No big deal."

"Surgery?" Andre hesitates with the bottle.

"Automatic and laproscopic. Surgery bots. No anesthesia. Super-science stuff. You know. Don't worry, I was unconscious." She wiggles the glass on the bar. "About that anesthesia—"

He doesn't fall for it but instead puts the bottle on the bar out of her reach. Vivienne starts to reach for it, but he touches her arm, freezing her in place.

"Talk to me," he says. "Tell me what's going on."

Part of her wants to tell him off—that it's just not his business—but she also knows that isn't true. For all the reasons Vivienne thought of before and because, fuck it, she can't do this alone. She called Wren, after all. She's already reached out, even if it obviously didn't go well. At least with Andre, she can feel his earnest need to comfort her—there's love there, and that's not something she gets to feel very often.

Round two.

"I'm in some shit, Andre," she says.

When he just nods sagely, she scowls.

"You don't have to look so smug about it, you smug motherfucker."

That makes him smile. And pour them both a scotch.

It feels good, getting it out there. The Orestes kid stalking her, the attack, the safehouse, all of it. Andre smiles at the mention of Angel—he's always liked Vivienne's niece, and never missed a chance to comment on the aesthetic quality of her music videos, the design of her costume, etc. It'd be cute if it wasn't so obviously an attempt to get them to reconcile, which had always seemed impossible, considering the whole "faked my death, now in hiding" thing.

Guess that's moot now.

"So," Andre says when she's done. "You think it's a coincidence?"

"Fifteen years after the Supergroup Massacre?" Vivienne shakes her head. "Someone's after me, and it's not the kid. He just got lucky, and he definitely didn't hire those ninja or the Pugilist. No, this is someone else."

"Someone else." A dark look crosses Andre's face, and he reaches under the bar to pull out the shotgun they keep there for emergencies. "Is it Raven?"

"*The* Raven, and fuck, I hope not." Vivienne downs her scotch and pushes out her glass for another. "Besides, if it was Tony, he wouldn't have missed."

"And he would have come himself," Andre says as he pours.

"Heh." Vivienne makes a face. "Flatterer."

"You tore out the man's eye," Andre says. "You don't think his hate-boner's lasted this long?"

"He should really get that checked out," Vivienne says. "By a therapist, I mean. Sex workers don't charge enough for that."

"Y'all need therapy," Andre says.

They both laugh. It reminds her of Wren, though, and how royally she fucked *that* up. She can feel Andre's ease and good cheer, but at least her empathy doesn't work the other way around.

It's a blessing and a curse—always knowing how other people feel, and always hiding how she feels.

As the mirth dies down, Vivienne looks back at the shattered mirror behind the bar, which shows about twelve versions of her bruised face with the butterfly bandage over her left eyebrow. They're all the same face, but the angle makes them look different. Some of them are angry, some sad, some determined. She brings the glass to her lips.

"What about the kid?" Andre asks.

Vivienne almost chokes on her scotch. That earns her a little side-eye from Andre, who sips his scotch in a knowing way.

"It's not like that," she says.

"Sure." He looks unconvinced.

"No, no," she says. "He's half my age, and besides, he's got powers."

"Like, *powers*, powers?" Andre raises an eyebrow. "What sort of powers?"

"The sort of powers you get if you're the illegitimate son of Justice." She drinks, and the scotch burns unpleasantly. "Those kind of powers."

"Wait, seriously?" Andre asks. "*Justice*, Justice?"

"Yeah, the big guy himself," Vivienne says. "There was this Supergroup mission to Tacoma, and Justice saved this accountant who was caught in the crossfire and—" She drinks the rest of her drink. "You know how it goes. There were late night visits. The rest of the team heard about the affair. He and my sister got divorced, it was a whole big thing."

"No shit." Andre pours the rest of the bottle, refilling their glasses.

"Those are both for me, right?"

He nods. "I was just a kid, but I remember when Justice and Athena broke up," he says. "It was a huge deal. You'd have thought the Queen of England broke up with the Prince. Front page news everywhere, every chat room exploding. There were all kinds of theories—the old thing about him being a space alien and he molted or something, or that she was a lesbian or something."

"My sister? Tsch, please." Vivienne drinks one of the scotches in one go. "He wanted to do the right thing, the big idiot," she says. "Marry this woman, settle down, retire from the caped life."

"Jesus," Andre says. "What happened?"

Her phone buzzes. Voicemail from a number she doesn't recognize. The last thing she needs is to talk to some telemarketer. Probably won a cruise or something. She turns her phone upside down on the splintered bar.

"She disappeared." Vivienne shakes her head. "Tony—he was The Raven by then—anyway, he tried to find her, but she was just gone. Some of us thought one of our rogues got to her, or something like that. Justice was real broken up about it. Put on a brave face, but he was never quite the same after that." She picks up the other scotch, but her stomach isn't so sure. "Especially since Tony thought she was pregnant. The asshole might be the King of Fucks, but he was a pretty good fucking detective."

"Jesus," Andre says again.

Her phone buzzes again, but she ignores it.

"So what are you gonna do?" Andre asks.

"Rebuild," Vivienne says. "Business as usual. Forget any of this ever happened. If The Raven's on to me, not a lot I can do about it. If I die, you get the bar."

Andre's face darkens. "We could run," he says. "I know some people in San Francisco. My ex lives down there. David's a good guy. You'd like him."

"Fun as it sounds to crash on the couch of a bunch of queens," Vivienne says, "that wouldn't do any good. I've already faked my death twice—I won't get away with it a third time. Unless Tony's become a complete idiot since I saw him last, he has images of my face from the security feeds in the safehouse. And with his temper, I don't think he'll stop tracking me until he personally dumps my corpse into a shallow grave full of kerosene and lights the match himself. Then stands and watches." She grabs the bottle and tops off her glass.

"Shit."

"Shit is right."

Her phone buzzes a third time, and that's about all Vivienne can take. She flips the phone over. "Three missed calls?" she says. "Who the fuck—?"

"I'll get us some food, ok?" Andre says. "At least the fight didn't make it to the kitchen."

Vivienne nods absently.

Each of the voicemails is only a few seconds long, and the phone reports the transcripts as "inaudible." She clicks one, and it's just heavy breathing. The *fuck*.

She's about to click the phone off and delete the messages when she hears it: a crackling, ragged voice that speaks a single word: "*Vivienne*."

The phone falls from her nerveless fingers onto the bar, where it sits quiescent for a second. Then it starts buzzing in another call. The same unknown number.

"V?" Andre asks from the back. "Everything all right?"

She ignores him and picks up the phone. It buzzes two more times before she answers.

"What."

All she hears is heavy breathing on the other end.

"You better tell me who you are, motherfucker, or—"

"Or what, Vivienne?" asks that same creepy voice. "You'll *punish* me?"

The voice sounds really familiar. She's dealt with her fair share of creeps and stalkers over the years, even after she went into hiding. An object lesson in how sexism has nothing to do with fame or popularity, and douchebags are ubiquitous and never-ending.

"Listen, you incel shit-fuck, I've had a really long day, so I'm going to make this easy," she says. "Don't call this number. Don't bother me again."

More breathing, increasingly heavy. "Are you sure? 'Cuz I—"

"Fucking *certain*."

She hits the red button and the call ends.

166

Vivienne barely has time to blow out a breath before her phone buzzes angrily. Same unknown number. She hits the green button but holds the phone away from her ear—a good idea, because what floods out is a string of curses and profanity. It's loud enough she might as well have the speaker on.

"Don't hang up on me, you fucking cunt! Do you have any *fucking* idea—"

She hits the red button again, cutting off the call.

Andre leans his head out of the kitchen, using a kerchief to wipe the sweat off his brow. "What was that, V?"

She waves him away.

A full minute passes before the phone rings again. It's that same number.

She almost hits "block caller," but something stops her. Her neck itches slightly, and she feels a faint twinge of dread. She can't shake the feeling this is all connected to what's been happening for the last couple days.

She answers on the fifth ring, and she holds it a foot from her ear. "Yeah?"

There's a sharp inhalation of air, but no more words. She turns on the speaker, but she still can't hear anything coherent. Whoever it is, he's hesitating.

"Look, you wanna talk, or what?" she asks. "I have a lot of drinking to do, so give me one good reason not to block this number—"

What she hears next is something she never could have expected. The phone fumbles a bit, and then a soft female voice speaks up. "Aunt V? Is that you?"

Immediately, Vivienne sits up ramrod straight and presses the phone to her ear. Her pulse quickens. "Angel? *Angel.*"

The sound shuffles again, and it's the creep's voice. "That got your attention, Vivienne?" he asks, extremely loud because the speaker's still on. "Glad something finally did."

She turns the speaker off and cradles the phone. "What do you want?" she asks, snapping her fingers at Andre. He wanders over, frowning.

"What? No threats?" The creep clicks his tongue. "No, 'oh no, don't hurt her'?"

"Listen, asshole, this isn't my first time." Vivienne puts the phone back on speaker on the bar. "Tell me your terms, and we'll see what we can do."

"That seems reasonable."

She gesticulates wildly at Andre, who finally pushes the mute button on the phone. "What can I do?" he asks, as the creepy dude is listing off demands.

"Can you trace this?"

Andre gives her a "seriously?" sort of look. "This isn't CSI."

"Just—do *something*."

"Vivienne," the voice says. "Are you there, Vivienne?"

"Yes!" she says, then louder. "*Yes!*"

"Vivienne?"

Andre sighs and turns off mute for her. He starts clicking on his own phone.

"Yeah, I'm still here, you shitgibbon," Vivienne says. "You just want to see me, right? That's what this is about?"

There's a pause, during which she strains to hear. "Yes," he says finally. "You know where to find me. Come alone, and if you're not here in an hour, they die."

"Fine."

There's a hesitation. "No begging me to wait? No more curses?"

"I'll need proof of life," Vivienne says. "Otherwise you're not getting what you want."

"Yeah, like this is *my* first time," he says, "oh, and wear the costume."

"Oh, fuck *you*."

"Now you're getting it." He hangs up.

Vivienne looks up to Andre, who stands behind the bar, tapping furiously on his phone. "Well?"

"I didn't trace it, if that's what you're asking. I'm contacting the police." Andre's fingers fly. "Best I could do was record it. It's a burner phone, probably."

"It's fine, I already know where he is."

Andre raises one eyebrow. "You do?"

Vivienne takes his phone and hits play on the recording. The same creepy voice comes through, slightly distorted and grainy, so she turns it up. Voices in the background, a distinct, shrill argument between two women. Voices she heard just an hour ago, back on Capitol Hill.

"What is that?" Andre asks.

"A lead." She looks up at him, and her eyes glimmer with purple flame. "Is my bike still here?"

Andre holds up her keys clinking on the ring.

28. POSTNASAL DRIP

When he wakes up, the first thing Marcus Orestes notices is intense congestion. He tastes snot and bile in his mouth and tries to cough it out, but when he draws in a breath, it just gets worse. Something wet and slimy is in his mouth, stuffed in there. He can neither spit it out nor swallow it, and instead he hangs there, choking, chest heaving.

He hangs there, because he's attached to the ceiling, staring down at the floor below.

He squirms, disoriented, but there's something holding him in place—something waxy, like half-dried glue, which smells and tastes like vomit. It holds his head rigidly in place, coating his whole body, his face, his mouth—it's down his throat. He can breathe, but only just, and it feels like he has to keep intentionally breathing in and out, like his lungs won't work if he doesn't make them.

Down in the living room, the lighting is dim, with just a little bit of afternoon light trickling between the blinds. The TV shows just a blank screen, with the mute icon bouncing from the corners. It crackles a bit, some of the color bars malfunctioning. Maybe something hit it? The table lies on its side, dumping all the comic books and old copies of the *Stranger* onto the shag carpet. Semi-hardened slime covers nearly every surface, dripping from the corner of the table and the couch.

A figure moves through the room, maybe three feet below him, muttering. He sounds like he's having a conversation with someone—himself, maybe? No, there's a phone cradled against his ear. And in his other hand, he's got—is that a gun? Yes. He's waving around a pistol.

"It's fine," he says. "I've got it handled. No, no—listen, it's fine. I just want to talk, that's all."

He sounds familiar, but Orestes's sluggish mind can't place him. He tries to speak and makes a muffled slurping sound.

"Look, I've—I said I've got it *handled*. It's fine. Hang—hang on." The man looks up at Orestes, eyes shining green in the flickering light. His face is contorted with what has to be utter madness, and he smiles right at Orestes. He has green muck smeared on his chin. "I'll call you back."

The phone beeps off, and the madman stands there contemplating Orestes's wild, terrified eyes, slowly turning his head from side to side. Sweat breaks out all over Orestes's body, making his skin itch as it mingles with the sticky stuff adhering him to the ceiling. The scrutiny lasts for what seems like an hour but is probably just a full minute. Which is an utterly inexplicable amount of time to just *look* at someone.

Finally, Orestes tries to speak, but the gunk in his mouth and throat chokes off any attempt. He thrashes, trying to scrabble at it, but his hands are just as secured to the ceiling.

"Now, now, Marcus." The man holds up one finger, instantly freezing Orestes in place. "I pasted you up there for a reason, and that was to keep you out of harm's way. I'd hate to have to hurt you."

Orestes tries to scream obscenities down at him, but the gunk won't permit it.

"What was that?" the man asks, cupping a hand around his ear. "You'll have to, *heh*, enunciate."

Orestes thrashes again, but abruptly the man leaps up onto him on the ceiling, arms and legs spread out to either side. He perches under Orestes like a spider, a praying mantis, or ...

An *Aphid*.

"I could, *heh*, ungag you," the Aphid says, sniffing at Orestes's neck. "But you have to promise not to scream. Also, you're not going to like when I put it back in. What do you say?"

Orestes nods as best he can, wide-eyed and terrified.

"Whatever you're into," the man says, then seizes a chunk of sticky material over his mouth and wrenches it away. His throat contorts and his body jerks taut as a long tentacle of semi-hardened snot snakes out of his mouth, and he gasps, sputtering and retching.

"There," the Aphid says, grinning madly, only a few inches from his face. "Always better not to talk with your mouth full, *heh*."

Only then does Orestes realize he knows this man. In another context, never moving like this, never grinning like a lunatic, but ... "Dr. Francis?" he asks, panting.

"Now, now, Mr. Orestes," he says, rubbing his nose against Orestes's face. "How many times have I told you to call me *Frederick*?"

His tongue flicks out and touches Orestes's ear, making him recoil. Then the Aphid springs down, laughing like it was some sort of joke.

"Seriously, though, Mr. Orestes," he says. "You should have seen your face. If it weren't covered in sap, anyway. Or even if."

"What the fuck, Dr. Francis?" Orestes squirms but still can't move. "You're the Aphid?"

"That's right, Mr. Orestes," the Aphid says. "Keep up."

Orestes goes through everything he knows about the Aphid from the comics. Junior Supergroup member, contemporary of Lady Vengeance, about ten years older than her. Missing, presumed dead, after the assault on Supergroup fifteen years ago, the Aphid's power-set included heightened reflexes, speed, dexterity, and the spontaneous generation of a fast-hardened compound he called his "sap." The comics, Orestes now realizes, never really captured exactly how gross it really is.

"Jesus," Orestes says, tasting vomit in his mouth—his own, and also the Aphid's, mingled. "This is your thing? Your *sap*?"

"My emission, yes." He looks mildly offended. "I haven't produced this much in years, *heh*, but I'm real excited."

"But—" Marcus's eyes widen. "Vivienne Cain."

"Lady Vengeance." Frederick Francis—the Aphid—shivers all over with a sick kind of pleasure.

It all makes a certain horrifying sense. The Aphid and Lady Vengeance were tied together for about a minute, though only a real comics geek would remember that. Aphid first showed up toward the end of the "Girl Vengeance" arc, when Vivienne Cain left Supergroup and joined the teen superhero group Agents of Awesome (AoA, for short), a transparent attempt to capitalize on the teen teams boom of the nineties; mostly it was about the whole team awkwardly flirting and kissing each other. No sex, but lots of make-outs.

The comics tried to make him a suave new love interest, after V's whole thing with the Shrike blew up (what was their name? They were named after a bird, he thinks). There was a thing, or at least the comics suggested the Aphid had a thing for Lady Vengeance, but there's only so much even the most talented writer can do to make adhesive vomit sexy, so the first issue of *A&V* bombed hard. The main Supergroup line went through its lowest-selling period until they axed the relationship and made V knee the Aphid in the balls, after which the Aphid became a comic relief sort of character. Romance comics were basically dead, and meanwhile, V moved on with the whole grittier, more mature Vengeance-Raven-Athena-Justice love quadrangle.

"I know what you're thinking," the Aphid said. "You're plumbing your geek archive—*heh, plumbing*—trying to figure out my weaknesses. But it isn't gonna work. You know why?"

Orestes coughs, trying to clear his throat. "Because you weren't in that many comics?"

"Exactly!" The Aphid spread his arms wide, encompassing the ruined apartment. "They made me a fucking *joke*. Supergroup sought me out—they came to *me*, not the other way 'round. I caught the New York Eviscerator, I beat the Piranha and the Spider Queen at the same fucking time! I was the Kurt Cobain of superheroes, not fucking *Mike Myers!*"

"Who?" Orestes asked.

"Fucking kids." The Aphid gave him a frustrated glare. "I was there first. I was going to be the main hero of the team. I was a goddamn rock star, and that bitch *ruined* me."

Orestes frowned. "You mean, like in the comics?"

He thought back to those issues. It was shortly after Supergroup volume 2, number 5, which the cover printed as the roman numeral "V" because it was the first appearance of Vivienne Cain in costume as Lady Vengeance, at least as part of the team. It's not really true that the Aphid predated her: she first appeared in volume 1, back when Azazel the Many-Mouthed Devourer took over Vivienne, Athena's kid sister. They kept her around the headquarters for a bit, and Aphid joined the team around the same time, replacing Antonio DeSantes as The Raven's sidekick. He made a pass at Vivienne, Orestes recalls, but she shut him down hard, which was the start of her popularity. She quit Supergroup and joined the Agents of Awesome, a teen capes team based in the Midwest somewhere, as "Girl Vengeance," and the comic outsold Supergroup for a while. Eventually, she rejoined Supergroup when she turned eighteen. Aphid was still on the team, but the damage had been done, and he was never a fan favorite after Vivienne rejected him.

Keep him talking, Orestes thinks. That's what he's read in the comics. You always keep the villain talking until help arrives.

"So you hate her," Orestes says, "because she was more popular than you?"

"Only because the comics made it look like that," the Aphid says. "That whore smeared my reputation and my good name, and for what? Just to humiliate me."

"Why?" Orestes asks. "Because you hit on her?"

"What?" The Aphid blinks up at him through goggling eyes. "No. No, Marcus, that's not how things went down. That's just the way the comics showed it. Fucking propaganda rags."

"So what happened?"

His big eyes gloss over, and he lounges back on the couch with a big, drawn-out sigh. It's this weird romantic gesture, like he's some kind of Byronic hero set upon by the cruelties of the world. He almost looks like a human being again, but the protruding gut stained with green vomit spoils the illusion. He looks off into the middle distance, remembering.

Orestes takes the opportunity to check on Angel, imprisoned just to his right. She hangs there limply, her vomit-sticky hair tumbling down around her face. Seeing her in that state makes him tremble, both out of a deep, gut-wrenching concern and also a burning hot coal of anger. He hopes she's all right, but if she isn't ...

"It was love at first sight, Marcus," the Aphid says. "I joined Supergroup when she was still on the AoA, you know. I never saw her as some kid, unlike everyone else on the team. They'd all fought her when she was a kid, when that demon took her over, but not me. Sure, she did all kinds of stupid things with the AoA, but when she showed up to join Supergroup, she was all *woman* to me. Not Athena's kid sister. Not the spoiled brat playing back up dancer for Robin fucking Electric Shock. Young, vibrant, and fucking in charge."

Gross.

"She was just eighteen," Orestes says. "You--"

"Exactly!" The Aphid says. "You know that barely legal pussy is the best. You know what I'm talking about, right? *Heh.*"

Orestes says nothing. He feels nauseated, and not just from the Aphid vomit.

"That's when all the trouble started," the Aphid says. "From day one, I made my interest clear, but she rejected me. Me, the up-and-coming star of Supergroup. Nah, she had to go for that cuck Tony DeSantes. *Fuck.*"

He spits vomit, the way someone else might hock up a ball of spit, and it lands on the coffee table in a big sizzling glop of yellow-green filth like a giant hairball. Steam comes off it, and in a few seconds, the safety glass cracks and shatters into a hundred chunks.

"Fuck man, I'm sorry," he says. "It's your place, I should be respectful. *Heh.*"

The constant "*hehs*" are a little weird and disconcerting. Orestes remembers Dr. Francis doing that a few times over the last few months, when he got really passionate in his lectures. A bit like other people say "um" or "like." If it was annoying then, it's disgusting now.

"Eventually I couldn't take it, the constant teasing," the Aphid says. "Can you really blame me? I'd catch a look when she was just getting out of the shower, or on a mission when she was putting on one of her sexy costumes, *heh*, and she'd never say anything or tell me to go away or anything. Just stare at me, you know?"

"And you'd have left her alone if she asked?" Orestes asks.

"Of course!" the Aphid says with a laugh. "Obviously. I was a nice guy. I was just trying to be nice, you know? She didn't have to be such a thirsty bitch about it."

"What do you mean?"

"She wanted it, obviously," he says. "And when she finally got it, she decided she was done with me. Reported me to the rest of the team. Tony even beat me up, that wetback fuck. Had to defend his property, of course. Sexist prick."

"He's sexist because he hit you?"

"Shit no." The Aphid rolls his big round eyes, which looks really unsettling, like a frog blinking. He barely looks human anymore. "Because he treated her like meat, and I was trying to sneak a bite. Fucking caveman behavior. And what did it get him in the end? Half-blinded by the same ungrateful cunt he tried to protect."

Jesus Christ, this guy. Orestes wants to vomit all over him.

He's about to say more, but the buzzer rings to signal someone at the door outside. For a second, Orestes's heart leaps, and he's sure it's Lady Vengeance coming to rescue them, or maybe some other superhero, or maybe just the police. But unfortunately, when the Aphid goes over to the door and presses the button by the display, the voice that comes buzzing through says, "Pizza for Marcus Orestes?"

"Come on up," the Aphid says at first, then, with a quick look around, he amends. "Actually, I'll be right down."

Dammit.

The Aphid clicks off the buzzer and turns back to Orestes. "I really appreciate you hearing me out, Mr. Orestes," he says. "We men have to stick together. These bitches think they can get away with anything."

Don't group me in with you, Orestes thinks, but doesn't have the courage to say aloud. Who knows what this incel is capable of?

He's about to respond, but then the Aphid hops in a forward flip and ends up perched under him like some sort of spider. That move alone startles Orestes, but his protest cuts off when the Aphid vomits all over his face, filling his mouth. The stuff tastes like bleach, and it burns all the way into his throat and lungs, hardening as it goes. He's choking, he can't breathe... and then it's the same as before, like being on a ventilator.

"Enough chat," he says. "Don't worry about a thing, my boy. I'll make that cunt pay. I promise."

Orestes tries to argue, but he can only gag on the disgusting stuff.

29. NO MORE RUNNING

Vivienne swings down from her motorcycle and stands outside the apartment complex she left just a few hours before. Under her leather jacket and sleek helmet, she wears one of her old costumes: the cleanest one she could find on short notice, hanging in a wedding dress garment bag in the back of her closet. It feels a little musty and more than a little tight, and she has the worst wedgie after riding all the way here up Denny, which she does her best to adjust, right there on the sidewalk. At least it's one of the updated ones and doesn't have the utterly impractical sideboob thing going on that was all the rage when she first started dressing up to fight crime. At least there's no cape, but if this is a sex thing, as requests for the costume usually are, this asshole's gonna be real disappointed.

Good.

"What's in your head, V?" she asks aloud. "Get in the game."

After today, she hopes he's not just disappointed but also in traction.

Yes, the voices say. *Drown him in your fury. Punish him.*

That. That's what's in her head.

Her head hurts, her hands shake, and her lips feel chapped. She needs a damn drink, but of course she can't have one. Not right now. If the asshole took out A-Girl, even with her powers compromised, then Vivienne needs her focus, and she needs as much power as she can muster. The alcohol might help with the voices, but it will do the opposite for those things.

She slides the claw out of the pocket on her bike and pulls it on slowly, thinking. If she goes up through the building, it gives her a chance to top off her emotional battery, and she might need every ounce of power she can absorb. But he's definitely going to be expecting that, and that'd be like walking right into a trap. She could try the window, though that would involve being able to guess which window is Orestes's apartment, and she's not even sure what floor it's on. Half the windows are lit up, half darkened, and it's not like she can easily fly up there and investigate. Dammit.

Nothing for it.

She strides boldly up to the front doors, wraps her clawed fingers around the handle, and—after a deep, centering breath—she pulls it open.

Or at least she would have, but of course it's locked.

She pulls twice to no avail and sighs.

"Dammit."

She ends up standing there, drumming her non-sharpened fingers against her black leather-wrapped thigh until two bubbly young women appear in the lobby, talking animatedly. She can feel their cloying enthusiasm from here, and almost wishes she were better at metabolizing inane joy. It's like a brain freeze. She pushes that away as best she can, pulls her phone out, and tries to catch their eye with little waves. A few awkward minutes later, one of them pushes the disabled switch and wanders over, expression furrowed.

Vivienne holds up one finger. "Oh, thank God, someone got the door," she says into the inactive phone. "Thanks! Ok."

She pretends to hang up and starts to head in, but the woman and her friend block the way, arms crossed. "I'm sorry, do you live here?" the blonde asks.

Really? Twenty-somethings, being responsible?

"Sorry, no." Vivienne puts on her best winning smile and slides the phone away into an inner pocket, revealing just a little hint of her costume. "I'm trying to be discrete, but I'm late for an appointment, and, well, this particular client doesn't like to be kept waiting."

One of them gets it, and her eyes widen. The other squints. "Client?"

"Uh." Vivienne only knows two dudes who live in the building, and one of them's definitely gay. "Marcus Orestes," she says, and tries not to wince.

"Marcus?" the brunette says, looking Vivienne up and down, from the black boots to the tights to the leather jacket and the hint of purple underneath. "What ... oh. *Oh*." They smile big.

"Right," Vivienne says. "Anyway, can I just—? Thanks so much."

They shift to the side and let her through. They wait at the still open door for a second while she heads to the elevator. It'd look weird if she took the stairs, obviously. She gives them another awkward smile, and finally they head out.

It's not the first time she's been mistaken for a sex worker, and odds are, it's not going to be the last. And there was that stint in 2005, and an argument could be made about the videos ...

"Marcus Orestes!" says the brunette outside.

"I knew he was a capechaser," says the blonde, as the door starts to close. "But hiring an escort? Wow!"

"Doesn't she seem, I dunno, like *older*?" asks the brunette.

"Yeah, but she's hot."

"He probably likes them that wa—"

Mercifully, the door closes, about the same time the elevator door opens. It's empty, and Vivienne steps inside. She takes a deep breath, looks upward, then pushes the button for the third floor, which she's pretty sure is right.

"Here we go," she says.

~

No sooner has Lady Vengeance infiltrated the building than an Uber pulls up outside and someone gets out. They're slightly under medium height, compact and wiry, with close-cropped dark hair and startling blue eyes that range from the absorbing to the determined, as now.

"Have a good day, Miss—I mean, Mister?"

"Doctor."

Wren shuts the door a little harder than they intended. Through heavy Seattle traffic, they've followed the triangulation on the call right here, to this apartment building in Capitol Hill, but only when they happened to look out the window and saw a hauntingly familiar figure in black leather on a motorcycle cruising between the cars in this direction did they know for sure they were doing the right thing. Wren might have thought nothing of the biker, but she left a distinctive purple energy trail in her wake, one that a normal person might have dismissed as a trick of the light. It's been over a decade, but Wren knows the look of empathic projection when they see it.

At that point, much as they hated it, Wren directed the driver to use the bike lane as necessary.

Definite moving violations and all, they still arrived at the coordinates a little too late. V's black and purple bike is there, tucked around the corner in the alley, but no sign of V herself. On their way to the door, Wren passes two college girls wandering past and talking about some boy with questionable tastes. They don't give Wren a second look, which is fine. It's about time for Wren to put their game-face on, and that leaves no time for unnecessary conversation. The messenger bag slung over Wren's back feels hot and heavy.

Why is Wren delaying? Does putting the mask on really fill them with that much trepidation?

Yes.

The door is the first obstacle, but Wren just pushes all the buttons in turn until someone buzzes them in. It's the sort of solution V would have thought of when they were kids, and that jabs Wren's mind with other memories. V getting them into a party they really shouldn't have been at, smiling that crooked little smile of hers, her purple eyes gleaming ... All things Wren worked hard to get through—to forget.

Wren sets their jaw as the door buzzes, takes a deep breath, then pushes their way in.

~

At the top of the stairs, and Vivienne faces the hallway she left that morning, with the same remnants of caution tape on the elevator doors. Her vague memory of heading down two flights of stairs has steered her right, which isn't a first, exactly, but it is rare. After a self-harming lifetime of demonic possession, alcoholism, and more than a few drugs, her memory lies to her as often as it tells the truth.

For years, she kept assuring herself and Andre that she was fine, but when she has to be honest, this last decade after the incident, she settled into a gray, disconnected haze, living through events only tangentially connected to one another. She watched her life, from the outside looking in, through a fogged window. She pounded on it occasionally—she was Lady Vengeance, after all—but mostly she didn't mind this glass prison. Every day was the same, punctuated only by different lunch specials Andre whipped up. She'd told herself she was content, but really, she'd given up, and she'd done it for so long, she convinced herself she hadn't. Now, pushing forty, she watched and waited for the day either her mind stopped working or her liver exploded. She'd lose that race either way, but she told herself it was fine.

This is fine.

Not anymore. As she walks toward the apartment at the end of the hall, she raises her arms slowly to draw the emotional energy from the apartments she passes into herself. Anger, frustration, stress, desperation, and deep, deep simmering rage with no outlet—all the worst, most destructive passions flow into her, empowering her, and purple energy dances around her hands and up her arms. Her claw trails along the wall to her left with a faint scratching sound. Power shapes around her, coalescing into bands of ghostly armor.

She isn't sure what changed. But it isn't just about her anymore—if she does nothing, she isn't the only one who will suffer. The kid, Marcus Orestes—he was the first crack in the glass, reminding her about sins past: mysteries and regrets, a life she could have lived, a life she could have watched her friends live. Angel was a second blow, confronting her again after all these years, watching her hurt and suffering. The darkness seeped like water through that crack, increasing its flow until it became a waterfall.

Now—standing before Orestes's apartment, fairly humming with power, cloaked in fear armor, extending her right hand to knock—the glass strains to the breaking point, and for the first time, Vivienne wonders why it ever felt so strong in the first place.

Because of me, the voice says. *Because you are afraid.*

No more running.

She knocks on the door, discharging a burst of fear energy, and it swings open as though not only unlocked but unlatched, striking the wall inside and shivers, the safety chain jangling freely. She might as well have bashed the door in with a portable battering ram. No attacker comes rushing out of the gloom, so she takes a breath and steps inside.

The place is a hollow mix of dark and crackling, static light from the buzzing TV, which is turned up just loud enough to be irritating but not go through the walls. A digital clock on the counter flashes with red light, revealing a filthy kitchen counter completely covered in rubbish: used pizza boxes, spilled food, and dirty dishes. The whole apartment reeks of bile and something astringent like bleach. The drapes are closed and the heater cranked up, filling the place with cramped humidity. It looks a little bit like a pad belonging to some bachelor who doesn't clean, doesn't bathe, and generally doesn't give a shit about anything other than playing video games all day.

Vivienne can see the obvious signs of a scuffle, though someone had put in a halfhearted effort to clean up: ripped couches and chairs were righted, and the shattered glass table in the living room has only part of one pane left in it, the broken glass swept up. If Vivienne already knew it was a trap, why the guy would sort of clean up after the fight is beyond her.

That is, until something wet and slimy drips onto her cheek, and she freezes in place. She knows who this is.

"Motherfucker," she says. "Really? *Really?*"

She doesn't even need to look up, but of course she does. There, plastered to the ceiling, hang Angel and Orestes, their bodies encased in hardened greenish vomit. Angel looks out of it, stringy hair hanging down around her sleepy face, but Orestes's eyes are wide open and terrified. He's trying to say something, but of course he's got the stuff in his mouth and throat. At least it conducts oxygen, but Vivienne has breathed that shit enough to know it's not remotely pleasant.

"Come out, Stevie," she says. "That's enough."

The faint droning buzz she couldn't pick out from the static rises and turns into words. "Stefan, babe," he says. "It's *Stefan.* You know that!"

The door slams shut behind her, plunging the room into mostly darkness, lit only by the static on the TV and the flashing power-interrupted clock. A spindly man with a prodigious beer belly stands on his hands, contorted oddly in the entryway, where he must have been clinging to the high ceiling. He's wearing, ugh, it looks like one of his old costumes, but it's obviously too small for his gut and too big for his arms and chest, so it hangs like unused skin around where all the muscle used to be. For one grotesque second, Vivienne sees the wiry warrior the man used to be, but it's all in the bent, insect-like posture, not in the shape of his actual body.

"Aphid," she says.

"Vengeance," he says, a little cheekily. The adhesive vomit drips from his mouth and he spits a globule on the floor. "*Heh.* Sorry. Where's my manners? And I tried to clean up for you."

Stefan Spencer's in his late forties but he looks at least fifty. He's bald in that shaved-headed white guy way, but she gets the sense he wouldn't have that much hair even if he grew it out. Thick jaw, decent cheekbones, but his face is slightly pinched, rodent-like, with heavy bags under his eyes. There's some attempt at a goatee, which only makes him look more douchey.

They face each other—him in the worn, ratty remains of his old costume, adhesive vomit dripping from his mouth, her cloaked in purple armor shaped of fear energy—and the silence draws out.

"Wish I could say it's good to see you, but it isn't," she says. "You know, you were the one member of Supergroup I hoped didn't survive? Also, you look like shit."

"*You* don't," he says. "Though it's hard to check you out through all that fear. Maybe you should drop it. Slip into something a little more, heh, *vulnerable.*"

Enough of this bullshit. She extends her clawed hand toward him, seizing his fear so she can end this. "Fuck you, you incel fu—"

But there's nothing. Just emptiness.

No ... a faint buzzing, as if from a barrier. He has protection from her powers, somehow. She can't even feel his emotions—that's how he was able to get the drop on her.

"Ah!" he says. "You think I wasn't prepared for your bullshit?" He raises his left hand, showing the ring on his ring finger. It's a gaudy thing with an aquamarine stone. "Not so much without your magic, *heh*, are you?"

Fuck, it's the fucking "*heh*." His nervous tic. Fuck this guy.

She doesn't need the magic. She's decked out in a full suit of fear armor with energy to spare, and she can just do to him what she did to the door. She takes a single step in his direction, and he flinches back, eyes wide, like she took a swing. He raises a matte black pistol to point at her.

"A fucking Glock?" She smiles with one side of her mouth. She definitely scared him. "You let me charge up enough to block a 50-cal shell, you utter moron. You think your little penis-substitute is going to scratch me?"

Rage spikes inside him, and his face turns from solicitous to furious in an instant. "Don't you talk to me!" Spittle flies from his mouth and sizzles on the wall and carpet. "Don't you talk like that to me, you fucking cu—" He clears his throat and points the gun not at her but up at Angel and Orestes, and that makes her wince. "Yeah, I fucking thought so, you bleeding-heart bitch."

Up on the ceiling, Orestes's eyes are wide and he's trying to shake himself free, but to no avail. That stuff is too hard for any baseline human to break.

"Stevie, this is about you and me," she says, trying to remain calm and, more importantly, keep him calm. "Leave them out of it. I'm the one you want."

"Yeah." His rage subsides somewhat, draining away into something much more lustful. "I'm glad you figured it out, *heh—heh*, you stupid whore. Now." He gestures to her. "Drop the armor."

"Fuck you."

He points the pistol up at the two on the ceiling. "Do it."

"Don't—" She raises her hands to ward him off. "All right, Steve. All right."

"*Stefan*," he says, settling into being in charge. "Get it right, bitch."

"Stefan."

With a deep breath, Vivienne releases the fear armor, and it spins crazily only to dissolve around her. She's a lot more vulnerable now, though with the residual fear energy, she could probably deflect a bullet or two.

186

"There she is." The Aphid rights himself and adjusts the spectacles hanging off his nose so he can look her up and down in her black V costume with the purple trim. "God, you're even hotter than you were in the last picture I had. You remember, the slutty burka costume? That was always my favorite."

Ew. "That was a niqab, you racist shit."

"Whatever." He gambols forward to scrutinize her more closely, his eyes bugging out a little, and he frowns. "Well, I mean, your tits are sagging a little, and there are more wrinkles. But it's ok, you're still fuckable if you leave the lights off."

Vivienne resists the urge to spit at him. He's got the power here, and it sucks.

"Now." He gestures to her left hand. "Take off the claw."

Dammit.

She unbuckles the gauntlet, and it clatters to the floor. Losing the armor was bad enough, but dropping the claw cuts down her tactical options considerably. The power is still there, but the claw lets her focus it—contain it. If she cuts loose now, the Aphid isn't the only one in danger.

It's weird, not to be able to feel his emotions. She definitely scared him, and she still scares him, but that's always been his thing: his fetish for strong women, and humiliating them. Fine. She can play along, if it keeps Angel and Orestes safe.

The Aphid smiles, pleased to be in control, and reaches down to adjust his crotch. He's getting off on this. *Puke.*

Fucking spoiled trust-fund frat boy—too small for the football team, but studied the humanities to seem sensitive. Constant victim complex. Vivienne forgot how much she loathed him, but mostly because she thought he was dead.

"How did you survive?" she asks, hoping to strike a conversational tone.

"What, *heh*, you mean when you tried to kill us all?" he asks.

"No, that—" Vivienne shudders, a cold spike of her own fear running right through her. She didn't expect that comeback. "That's not what happened."

Yes, the voice says. *Yes, it is.*

Dammit, he shook her up. She was keeping the demon at bay, but now it feels like something broke inside her, and now there's nothing keeping it penned up.

"You never gave a shit about any of us," the Aphid says. "With your little nicknames and your superiority and shit. Always above us, always better than us, *heh*, no matter how many tattoos you got or how many assholes you slept with or the sex tape or how many drugs you shoved in your tramp face. *Heh*." He grins maniacally. "What was that nickname you had for me? You know the one."

"Suh," she says. "Slimeball."

"*Heh*," he says. "*Heh heh*, oh that's great. *Slimeball*. You fucking cunt."

Vivienne doesn't know what to say. Something is burning in the back of her head, and her whole body is pumping with rage and pain.

"Relax," the Aphid says. "I hold no grudges. I love you, after all. So what if you had a little psychotic demon break and murdered all our friends?" He grins widely. "Well, except Tony. I heard you tore his eye out with the claw. Priceless. *Heh*. Classic V." He presses the pistol to his face, covering one of his eyes, and mimes screaming. "Only way, *heh*, only way it would have been better is if you were fucking that piece of shit while you did it." He bucks his hips lewdly. "Surprise, bitch! *Heh*!"

He laughs at his own joke, and Vivienne risks taking a step toward him. He's sadistic and cruel, like always, and he seems to hate Tony as much as ever. She can't manipulate him directly, but maybe she can use that.

A pathetic waste of a man, the voice says. *Unfit to stand before you. He must die.*

"No." Vivienne shakes her head. "You—"

"What?" The Aphid cocks his head to the side. "What about me?"

"You were always jealous," Vivienne says, improvising. Much as she fucking hates this piece of shit, she can empathize. She can feel his jealousy, hot and choking, and she can use it against him. "I see that now."

"Jealous? Fuck you," the Aphid says, leveling the gun at her again. "You and Tony both. Him for being the self-righteous shit he always was, *heh*, and you for picking him, rather than a nice guy like me. Did you think you could just get away with that? That no one would hold you fucking accountable?"

It's only when he rants that she notices the faint accent, something he always hid when they were younger. Canadian? Fucking shame. Most Canadians she's met are lovely people.

She doesn't care about all the blather. She wants his attention on her, not on her niece and the kid. Power drainers are notoriously unpredictable, so who knows if Angel can take a bullet right now. Orestes, well, he's just a guy—not bulletproof even at the best of times, unless he has more power than she thought. That's a hell of a long shot, and she doesn't feel up to rolling those dice right now. This fucking sadist likes to feel in charge, and right now, he basically is.

"Is that what this is about?" Vivienne asks. "Holding me accountable for, what, fucking the hot guy? I've seen your dick, Stevie—unfortunately—and it's nothing to Tony's. That man— mm." She fakes a shiver. "Sorry, what was I saying?"

"Oh, you fucking bitch," he says, because he's such a nice guy. "To think I ever loved you."

"You *loved* me?" She laughs. "That's what you call sticking your dick in my face? You tried to *rape* me, you fucking shitstain—"

"You goddamn tease, you know you wanted it."

That's too much. Too fucking much.

Too much, the voice says. *Kill him.*

Maybe the voice has a point. She doesn't need the claw. She doesn't need any fear energy. Just her own strength. Vivienne steps forward, ready to throttle this misogynist shit with her bare hands.

"Hold it!" The pistol points up at Orestes and Angel again. "Not one more step."

She stops, wincing inwardly. Fuck.

What are you doing? the voice asks in her head. *You are a warrior. Strike him down, and leave these fool children. They deserve death as much as he does.*

"Shut up," she says under her breath, but only loud enough that the Aphid can just hear it.

"You think I don't know what you're doing?" he says. "You must think I'm pretty fucking stupid."

"Well—"

"Take off the jacket."

She gives him a dubious look but does as he asks, revealing her heavily tattooed arms, all the thorns glowing with absorbed power

189

that could crush him like, well, an aphid. The freight train full of dynamite bearing down upon him isn't what he staring at, though.

"And the shirt. *Heh.*"

"What?" She makes an utterly disgusted face at him. "Fuck. No."

It's not just about being in control. He's got to demean her. Because he's such a *nice* guy.

Kill him, the voice says, louder and more insistent. *Kill him.*

"Hurry up," he says.

"Just ... right here, in front of my niece?" she says. "C'mon, Stefan. Even you—"

"You show me your tits right now, cunt, or those kids are fucking dead," he says.

Vivienne's eyes burn with purple energy. "You touch those kids, and I will end you."

It's not entirely her voice.

"Or I'll get away, *heh*, like I did last time you tried to murder me," he says with a wicked smile. "You wanna, *heh*—you wanna roll those dice?"

The phrasing catches her like a shock of cold water to the face. Can he hear her thoughts? Telepathy was never in his power-set, not that she knows of. But he seems smarter than she remembers. And he's right—slippery little asshole is way faster than she is. He could kill both the kids before she lays a finger on him, and probably her too. Fuck.

Kill him. Kill him.

She reaches one tentative hand up to the strap of her tank top. She trembles, in fury and in fear.

The Aphid smiles big, and green drool drips from his mouth over his chin. "That's it," he says, wiping the sizzling vomit away. "Slow. And get on your knees, *heh*, that too."

KILL. HIM.

Yes.

That's when there's a knock at the door.

It's jarringly sudden but rather polite, this knock. Not the way neighbors would bang on the wall to get someone to quiet down, and the yelling has been loud. Vivienne pauses, halfway to the floor, and the Aphid perks up, eyes bugging.

"Over there," he says, gesturing, and she settles to a kneeling position mostly behind the couch, so she can barely see the door. "Don't you fucking move."

Seeing her in place and quiescent, he heads into the short entryway, making sure he has a line on his hostages. Vivienne looks up at Orestes and Angel, both of whom are awake now. Considering the grotesque situation, Angel seems to be taking it fairly well, looking down at Vivienne with determined eyes. By contrast, Orestes is practically hyperventilating, and it's only the gross vomit that's keeping him from passing out. He can't breathe right with that stuff down his throat. Vivienne is sympathetic, but all she can do is absorb some of the fear rolling off him. Slowly, he relaxes to a kind of quiet calm. Her powers don't affect everyone like that—she can usually only share someone's fear, not take it away entirely. Especially not someone who clearly has an anxiety disorder: such people are like a bottomless well of energy for her.

The Aphid stalks toward the door and looks out the peephole. "What is it?" he asks, his voice going from nice-guy-rage slurred to affable, even perky.

"Excuse me," says a soft, high-pitched voice from out in the hall. "My name is Dr. Fulcrum. I'm looking for an old friend."

Vivienne's eyes shoot to the door. She knows that voice—has heard it modulate—and if it's on the femme end of the spectrum, and the fake name, that means ...

"Fulcrum." The Aphid furrows his brow at the name. "Sorry, ma'am—I think, *heh*, I think you've got the wrong place."

"Doctor," the visitor says.

"I'm sorry?" the Aphid says, a touch of irritation in his voice.

"It's fine. Sorry to bother you."

Finally, Vivienne gets it. It's a signal.

The Aphid heads back over, shaking his head. "Stupid bitch," he says. "Where were we? Oh right." He lays the gun against her face, teasing the barrel down her cheek and over her lips. "I can't tell you how much I've looked forward to this." With his free hand, he fumbles at his belt. "I think I'll make you—"

The knock comes again, just as polite as before, and it gives the Aphid pause. "What the fuck!" he says, barely able to slur the words through a mouth full of expectant vomit.

"It's no big—"

She starts to speak, but he slaps her across the face with his free hand. It doesn't really hurt—she's taken a lot of hits, and Aphid isn't even in the top fifty—but it's startling enough that she trails off, coughing. Blood pools over her split lip, and she can feel a trickle of wetness down her cheek, and she realizes that not only did he break open her lip, that fucking ring cut open her face.

"Don't you fucking move," he says, and starts heading toward the door.

This isn't the time to stay still, though, and Vivienne tenses, ready to move.

The unlatched door explodes into the apartment as the Aphid approaches, startling him back, and a figure in white and black launches themselves through. The gun goes off with a thunderous crack, but the intruder twists away as though they knew where to dodge, so the bullet misses the white and black motorcycle-style helmet by a good twelve inches. One booted foot catches the Aphid's hand, knocking the weapon clattering away. He staggers back, and his attacker presses, flipping forward to bring both feet at their target—one into his chin, the other into his chest. As he falls back, green spittle flying, Vivienne sees her own purple glow reflected in the attacker's black visor.

"Fuck!" The Aphid shouts. "What the fuck—!"

The Shrike doesn't respond, but instead heaves themself up, runs along the wall, and aims a scissoring kick right at the Aphid's head. This time, though, he's prepared, and age and too much cheesecake haven't robbed him of his heightened dexterity. He ducks under the attack and lunges for the gun, but the Shrike is on him, sweeping his legs and sending him staggering. He's right back up, though, rolling away and hissing.

Vivienne doesn't need an invitation. She shoves herself to her feet and looks up at Orestes and Angel. Her niece is squirming, trying to break free, and the hardened vomit starts to crack. Is her super strength back? Orestes is just hanging there, trembling. He's paralyzed with fear, and it wasn't even Vivienne's power that did it. Dammit.

A tiny flash of blue lightning extends from Orestes, smashing into the TV, and its screen explodes in a shower of sparks.

"Fuck!" the Aphid is shouting. "Fucking fuck!"

LIBATIONS FOR THE DEAD

Vivienne is too short to reach Marcus, and the table is broken, so she shoves the useless TV off the entertainment stand and drags that over. It's much heavier than she expected, but she still has enough fear energy strength to manage it. Finally, she climbs on top and can just reach him, with their heads about able to touch. His pulse is elevated, his breathing too fast, and his eyes hardly seem to see anything. He's having a panic attack, and she can't blame him one bit.

"Hey," she says. "Hey. Marcus. It's ok."

His eyes blink and look first to her—she can see the whites all around the irises—then to the Shrike and the Aphid wrestling and darting around each other like furious jungle cats. She gets it, of course: most people have never seen two agility- and reflex-enhanced combatants, both of whom have at least some sort of precognitive ability, really going at each other, and even for Vivienne, it's hard to describe in any way other than watching an intricately choreographed dance on fast forward.

The Aphid may have acted like a damn fool with Vivienne, but when the fight gets real, he rises to the occasion, flailing viciously and with brutal accuracy. The Shrike, on the other hand, fights methodically, efficiently, and nearly perfectly. And that might be enough, but the Aphid fights dirty—always has. The second the Shrike falters in a step, the rug slipping under their foot, the bastard hocks up a massive hunk of vomit that narrowly misses the slender black-and-white wrapped body and melts a hole in the couch. The Shrike cries out in pain as trailing streamers of vomit eat right through their costume to reveal a stretch of muscular midsection.

"Marcus!" Vivienne closes her hands around Orestes's face. "Be here, with me. I need you."

His eyes lock on hers, and his fear floods into her, like a waterfall of molten chocolate or a line of cocaine. She's done a lot of drugs in her life, but this one is something else. She's trying to remove his fear, but it just overwhelms her, leaving her high and floating. Who is this kid?

Behind her, Vivienne hears the Shrike gasp in pain, and the Aphid cackles in glee. They put an end to that, though, putting a lucky kick in his stomach, and he descends into wheezing and gasping. "Goddammit!" he says, coughing. "C'mere, you little—"

Angel has broken one arm free, Vivienne sees, and she uses it to pull the gunk out of her mouth and throat. "Marcus!" she says.

His wide eyes dart to her, and just like that, Vivienne can feel the edge slip off his fear, and the panic settles a little.

"I'm going to pull this out," Vivienne says, taking hold of the mass of vomit and snot shoved into his mouth like a gag. "I'd say it's not gonna—" Then she channels fear energy and just does it, wrenching hard. Orestes's body goes taut, and he vomits some of his own, but at least she pulls it free. He hangs there, gasping.

"Oh God," he says. "Oh God, I'm going to die. I'm going to die—"

At that moment, the Aphid shrieks "bitch!" at the top of his lungs behind them, and a bullet slashes over her shoulder, just barely missing her head.

There's another shot, but Angel is there, hovering between the gun and the others, and the bullet bounces off her chest and ricochets into the ceiling. The Aphid unloads two or three more shots, but Angel blocks each one, grunting at the impact.

"No," Orestes is saying. "I can't—I can't—"

"It's all right," Vivienne says, touching his cheeks. "Hey. Look at me. Hey."

Not knowing what else to do, she draws his face toward hers and kisses him on the lips.

30. SHOCK AND AWE

Over the many ages of humanity, there have been great and legendary kisses: kisses that have launched wars or ended them, kisses that have capped off wild and fantastic tales, kisses that have awakened the dead.

This is not one of those. In the passionate and storied history of the art form, this particular kiss hardly warrants an awkward footnote.

It tastes like blood and bile, not least of all because one of the participants has, until recently, been breathing through a tentacle of hardened vomit. His lips are cold and clammy, hers split and speckled with blood. It's not great for either of them.

That said, it does the trick and snaps Orestes out of his panic. The voice screaming at him that he's going to die abruptly goes silent, and he looks down at Lady Vengeance who—oh my God—just kissed him. What is even *happening*?

The fear, it just drains away—out of him and into her. Her body shivers, and he can see she's having as much trouble focusing on the world around them as he did just a moment ago.

"Sorry," he says, because that's the only thing he can think of to say.

"I've had worse." Her eyes look dreamy. She brushes his forehead gently. "We'll try again later."

"Wait—*what?*"

"Aunt V!" A-Girl, floating between them and the gun-toting Aphid, little holes in her borrowed tee shirt, grunts in pain as another stray bullet bounces off her. She reaches and scrabbles at a chunk of Aphid vomit attaching Orestes to the ceiling. "Whatever you're gonna do, now would be good!"

195

Beyond her, the Aphid and that other cape—the Shrike—are fighting like two hurricanes, with the occasional bullet zinging out to hit the protective A-Girl. Orestes thought the Shrike retired years ago, but there they are. The Shrike catches the Aphid's hand up high and swats it with their other hand, knocking the weapon skittering away, but the Aphid smashes a push-kick into the Shrike's face to drive them back into the hall. The Shrike skids, arresting their fall, then reverses and leaps into the bathroom, where Orestes hopes they just dove into the bathtub, because the Aphid produces a submachine gun from somewhere and sprays bullets through the wall. Shell casings rain around the room, then he turns the weapon on A-Girl. The bullets bounce off her, shredding the tee shirt, but she grits her teeth at every impact.

He should be afraid, but all the fear has drained out of him, like it did in the Supergroup hideout. When Lady Vengeance fed on him. Is that what she's doing now? She doesn't look at all concerned.

"He's too fucking fast." Lady Vengeance turns her blood-stained face back to Orestes, her eyes glowing with mischievous purple light. "You're gonna have to zap him."

"Zap him?" Orestes asks, not understanding.

"You know," she says with her crooked smile. "Like a bug zapper."

The Aphid's SMG clicks empty, and he curses. He ejects the empty magazine and produces another out of somewhere—his pants, maybe?—and pops it in. He starts to move, maybe to get a shot around A-Girl, but the Shrike appears out of nowhere, costume torn and scuffed and smeared with scalding vomit, and launches a flying knee right at his face. He leaps back, managing to dodge enough that the Shrike only gets him in the chest, but he twists around and under them in midair so that they fly apart. The Aphid aims the SMG at their back, but the Shrike kicks off the ceiling and hurtles into the kitchen, narrowly managing to cover behind the refrigerator before bullets smash into it.

With all his fear gone, Orestes watches it with a detached, mechanical clarity. The Shrike is using good harrying tactics, but they're tired. They don't have much energy left. The Aphid, on the other hand, seems to have unlimited energy, fueled by rage. That's

196

going to provide the needed edge. He's going to kill all of them, or worse.

"Now would be good, Orestes," Lady Vengeance says. Her voice has a dreamy quality to it, and Orestes wonders if she's high. What kind of hit did she get off him?

"I don't—I don't know how," he says.

"Yes, you do." Lady Vengeance smiles encouragingly. "You've always known."

He frowns. "What does that mean?"

"I dunno," she says. "It just seemed like the right thing to say—"

Then, as if that weren't weird enough, she boops his nose and giggles to herself.

This isn't good.

Electricity crackles around him, sparking to the various electronics in the room, but he can't remotely control it. It seems far away. His mind recognizes what's going on, but his body senses no peril. He feels no sense of urgency, even though he recognizes the danger.

His eye burns, showing him what he needs to know.

His power. When did he use his power? In the graveyard, he fought his way through Lady V's curse, and then again in the bar. He used it in The Raven's warehouse, when he thought he was going to die. Even when he was nervous about interacting with A-Girl, it came out of him. And in all those situations ...

It's the fear.

The Aphid's SMG clicks empty, and he hurls it aside with a curse. A-Girl, floating there, her clothes shredded and her body a mass of bruises, smirks down at him. "That all you got, Uncle Stefan?"

With a hiss, he crouches, then springs at her like a lunging spider. She screams in surprise as he lands on her, adhesive vomit spraying from his mouth—she manages to avoid the worst of it, mostly by turning her face, but it still gets all over her. His weight and her waning focus let him bear her to the ground, where they splinter the entertainment cabinet under Lady Vengeance's feet. She falls and lands heavily on the floor amongst the broken glass and splintered wood, not too far from A-Girl.

"Ow," Lady V says, then starts giggling.

197

As both women lie there, stunned, the Aphid rolls on top of Lady V and puts his hands around her throat. Her laughter cuts off and her eyes go wide.

"Fucking bitch!" he screams as he chokes her. "Fucking bitch!"

She flails ineffectually, too high on fear energy even to fight back.

Watching it all from a detached emptiness, in that moment, Orestes understands what he needs.

"V," he says, and her rolling eyes focus on him. "Give it back."

It's not a well-articulated plan, but she seems to understand on some level, or maybe it's something else. Either way, she extends her hand toward Orestes, and purple energy swirls around her hand. He just—he has to reach it.

He strains against the gunk encasing him, holding him against the ceiling. When he and Chuck were super stoked about the high ceilings in this building, they couldn't have foreseen this particular drawback. A-Girl already broke off part of the sticky vomit and he manages to get his left arm free, but strain as he might, he can't make any more of it budge. His whole torso is trapped, and his abs are burning from the strain of trying to break through. Their hands—his grasping, hers limply reaching up—are still five feet apart.

"Goddammit, come on!" he says. "Almost—"

Lady V's hand starts wilting, fingers curling limply, as her strength fades. On the floor, she shudders, her body gasping and failing to get air. The Aphid snarls, drooling all over her.

"Come on!" Orestes prays. "Please!"

And an angel answers.

A-Girl appears between them, floating a foot off the floor. She takes Orestes's hand in hers, and she feels warm and solid. She looks up at him, smiling faintly. She believes in him, every bit as much as Lady Vengeance.

Then, with her other hand, she takes her aunt's hand, and jerks instantly taut as though she touched a live wire.

Purple energy shoots through A-Girl, burning like fire under her skin and bursting around her body. It's way, way more powerful than anything Orestes has felt or seen before. Is that *his* fear? All of his own fear, pumped into someone else. A-Girl contracts, curling into herself, and terrified sobs come out of her.

198

In the bar, she didn't react this way—she just collapsed—and his heart shudders to see her in torment like that. Is this what it's like to see him tortured by his anxiety?

Then the fear goes through her and into him. It doesn't hit him like a bolt of lightning, like it did A-Girl, but instead settles into him like an old friend cozying up on a cold night, sinking his fingers deep into Orestes's sore muscles and kneading. It feels slightly uncomfortable, but right at the same time. Until just now, he didn't realize how hollowed out he felt without the fear, but now it melds with him, and they become one. He feels bloated, as if maybe she put more into him than she pulled out, but either way, all the familiar fears and anxieties come back. His place in the world, his mother the stranger, his father he never knew ...

The Aphid shouts some expletive and kicks A-Girl away to slam into the wall, where she puts a crater in the drywall.

No more.

Orestes is on a path to resolve all this—to find himself—and now this misogynist motherfucker wants to put a stop to all that, starting with murdering the closest thing he's got to a guide to this nonsense. And next, that same incel douche canoe will murder the girl he kinda likes.

Hell *no*.

The anxiety fuels his powers, and a flood of blue-white lightning crackles around him. He's never had control of it before, and he doesn't really this time, either, but he doesn't have to. All he's gotta do is point himself at the problem.

The adhesive vomit bubbles and crackles and melts off him, and he falls down into the room. The power catches him before he hits the floor though, and he floats, buoyant, over the destroyed entertainment cabinet, lightning arcing in every direction. The Aphid looks up from the limp, unmoving Lady Vengeance, eyes bugging at Orestes as he hovers before him, lightning dancing around his body.

"What now?" he asks, his mouth sloppy with green bile.

"*Justice*, motherfucker," Orestes says.

The Aphid makes a move, trying to leap away, but even he can't dodge a force of nature. Every window in the apartment shatters as blue-white electricity thunders from Orestes's hands and catches the Aphid in a storm of crackling fury. He screams, but the shock cuts off the sound, and the energy blows him against the far wall, near the dropped pistol. The Aphid goes for it, just as Orestes lands on the floor and sweeps his arms across with a grunt. The electricity plucks up the Aphid, like an insect caught up in a current, and hurls him bodily across the room.

"Fuck *off*."

With a roar, Orestes takes two running steps and flings the Aphid right out the shattered window. The gun goes off, not quite as deafeningly loud with the windows broken open, and the Aphid goes flying out into the gathering dark. Orestes catches a last look at his panicked face as he goes out, eyes goggling, and remembers that the Aphid can't fly.

There's a loud crash from below, and Orestes looks down to see the Aphid lying in a shallow crater in the roof of an SUV. He twitches a little, but otherwise he's down for the count.

Lightning dances around the room for a hot second, making the TV crackle and pop again for good measure, then falls quiescent around them. All is silent: Orestes standing there, Lady V on the ground, A-Girl coughing and getting up. The Shrike comes limping out of the hallway, clearly favoring one leg, their costume a ripped, smoking mess.

"Jesus," A-Girl says. "You *do* have powers."

Then every fire alarm in the building goes off all at once, followed shortly by the sprinkler system.

The water flows over Orestes's head, washing away the residue of the Aphid's vomit. He lets it wash over him, purifying him, and breathes deep. Angel stares at him, water soaking her as well. She scrutinizes him carefully, considering.

"V!" comes a strangled voice. The Shrike rips off their scorched helmet and hurls it onto the remains of the couch, then rushes to Lady V's side. Beneath the mask, their face is angular and worried, with heavy black shadows around the eyes, and their nose is bleeding—probably from that kick to the face. Their black hair is tied up messily and hastily, some strands having come free in all the fighting. Under the mask, the Shrike looks sort of like an androgynous version of the actress from that one movie that came out around the time he was born. What was the name of that movie?

"Dr. Fulton?" Orestes asks. "That—that makes sense."

200

"Who?" Angel asks.

"I already called 911 before I came in." Wren ignores him and kneels beside Vivienne, touching at her face. In efficient order, they put their ear to her chest, listen at her mouth and nose, then gently touch her neck. "She's not breathing," they say with a grim expression. "You. I need you to direct the paramedics."

Angel stiffens. "We, uh, blew up every phone."

Wren sighs. "You can fly, right?"

Angel brightens, as though in the chaos, she'd forgotten all about that. "Right!"

Angel hurries over toward the window, where Orestes can already hear sirens and see flashing blue and red lights. She levitates a little—makes sure she can still fly—then steps out into the night.

Orestes frowns in thought. He knew Wren Fulton, child of the original Shrike, is non-binary, but this person seems pretty masculine. Very authoritative and gruff. Clearly accustomed to command, though that tracks—they did lead the Agents of Awesome.

"You," they say, and he snaps to attention. "What's your name?"

"Orestes," he says. "I mean, Marcus. Marcus Orestes."

"Ok, Orestes," Wren says. "You can control that electricity?"

"I—" Orestes finds himself nodding, though he's not sure it's true. "I can try."

"Good enough." Wren points to two spots on Vivienne's chest, just above her right breast and under the left one. "Shock her."

"I'm not a defibrillator," Orestes says, but Wren's glare brooks no argument.

He kneels and lays his hands on Vivienne where the doctor indicated. She doesn't feel cold yet, but neither does she feel like a living person. His heart leaps, but that's the only one. He doesn't produce so much as a spark.

"What are you waiting for?" Wren asks.

"It's not—it's not that easy." Orestes grits his teeth.

They glare at Orestes, and his face feels hot even as his body feels cold. Apparently, Vivienne taught Wren a thing or two about intimidating people during their shared time in the Agents of Awesome.

He feels the power surge within again, and he directs it through his hands, hoping he doesn't fry Vivienne—

All of a sudden, she gasps for breath and her eyes fly open. She arches back on the floor, her hands flailing, and Wren catches her in their arms. "Jesus," Wren says, their voice suddenly much softer, more feminine. "Jesus Christ, stop doing that."

"Wren?" Vivienne looks up at them through rolling eyes. "Oh shit."

"Oh shit is right." Wren leans in and kisses Vivienne, hard and fast, then pulls away, the better to shake her, the way one might an incorrigible puppy. "The fuck was that?"

"Ow," Vivienne says. "Gentle, Birdie. I just died, you know."

"Oh, I know." Wren takes a deep breath as though to shout, then expels it in a sigh. "God, I'm so mad at you right now."

"So what else is new?"

"Just—" Wren inclines their head, touching Vivienne's forehead with their own. "Shut up."

For once, Vivienne doesn't have a smart-ass remark to make, but just smiles and closes her eyes.

Orestes stands there, dumbfounded and increasingly feeling like a third wheel, until glass crinkles and A-Girl comes swooping back in, her flight barely controlled. She lands badly, skidding to a halt and nearly crashing into him. He catches her awkwardly, and they end up in each other's arms. After a little hesitant fumbling, they push apart again, all tension-diffusing smiles and coughing.

"They're on their way!" she says. "I directed them this way. Not that they needed me, I mean, there *is* a big electrical burn on the side of the building. That's—yeah." She trails off, seeing the little intimate moment between Wren and Vivienne. "You're welcome?"

The two grown-ups don't seem to notice her.

"Your, uh, powers aren't back to normal, huh?" Orestes asks.

"What?" Angel looks over at Orestes and blushes slightly. "Oh, uh—"

"No." Vivienne coughs and looks over. "No, she's always that clumsy."

"Oh, good to see you're fine, Aunt V." Angel rolls her eyes.

"Aunt—" Wren's eyes widen. "My God. Angel. You're so big."

"Uh ..." Angel blinks rapidly. "Wait. Titi Wren? Is that you?"

The two of them hug.

"Yep." Vivienne coughs again. "You want to, uh, maybe put some clothes on, eh, Angel?"

"Oh?" Angel looks down at the remains of the Supergroup tee shirt she borrowed from Chuck, which is little more than a rag sort of wrapped around her top. She had pajama pants once upon a time, too. "Oh."

All of which Orestes didn't notice. Nope, not even a little bit. Well ...

He's about to do something about it when the door creaks open at the end of the short hall and he looks up, expecting paramedics or cops with drawn guns or possibly the Emerald Legion.

Instead, Chuck stands there, holding two canvas bags full of groceries, which immediately tumble out of his hands onto the scorched floor. He stares at them, open-mouthed, and them at him.

Joy washes over Chuck's face. "Awesome!"

EPILOGUE: FLYING

Fifteen minutes later, they load Vivienne, strapped onto a gurney, into an ambulance. She's hooked up to a heart monitor and an IV, as apparently, she was very dehydrated, probably from all the booze. The police have already read her the list of Miranda rights, over Orestes's objections, but both Wren and Vivienne herself stop him.

"I've been a fugitive from justice for a decade, kid," Vivienne says, her voice hoarse. "There's some legal stuff that has to happen." She looks over at Wren. "And I'm done running."

Dr. Fulton returns the smile. Having changed from their torn costume into the well-fitted suit they wore on the way over, they've treated the cops in a masculine way, which makes sense—men with authority always seem to listen better to other men with authority—though the shift is subtle enough most people probably assume they present that way all the time.

"I'm licensed to practice law in the State of Washington, so there's no need to worry," Wren says. "Seattle is a sanctuary city. If you had to pick somewhere to come out of hiding, you could have done worse. There'll be an investigation, but the case is weak. I've looked into it." They flush a little. "I had some free time."

"Not a lot of work for shrinks in the Midwest?" Vivienne asks.

"Mental health workers," Wren says, correcting her. "And you'd be surprised." They look irritated, but in a familiar way. "And if you must know, it was mostly research I did at the time of the attack, and then on the flight. I passed the bar years ago."

"How many degrees do you have, Doctor?" Orestes asks.

"Five," they say. "Psychology, Law, Physics ..."

"Say, Birdie, I'm in a lot of pain ..."

205

"Not that kind of doctor, V."

"Damn."

"I've got to talk to the officers," Wren says, touching Vivienne gently on the arm. It's a very femme sort of gesture. "You're going to be all right?"

"I think we both know the answer to that, Birdie."

Wren returns a wry smile and kisses Vivienne on the forehead, then heads off, back in full masc mode to deal with the cops.

Vivienne blows out a long sigh and winces. "That wasn't just drug-seeking behavior," she says to Orestes, her words rasping. "I really am in a lot of pain."

"Sorry." Orestes starts to move away, but she grabs his hand, and their eyes meet. Her bruised and bleeding face is determined.

"No more running," she says. "For either of us."

Lightning crackles around Orestes—just a little, enough to make the instruments in the ambulance protest, squawking and beeping. He gets it back under control though, and nods. "Yeah."

Orestes looks at the cops wrangling the mostly unconscious Aphid—Dr. Francis or Stefan or whatever his name really is—into the back of a black anti-powers van. The lights inside flicker with the distinctive green light of power drainers. Wren was right: Seattle isn't known for cracking down on capes, though Orestes suspects this incident might change things a little. There'll be more pressure, and a fight. It seems to be one Vivienne doesn't mind, though.

Dr. Fulton comes back, exchanges words with the medical attendants, then climbs in the ambulance with Vivienne. Orestes's last sight of the battered Lady Vengeance, she's smiling and looking determined.

"Hi." Angel wanders over, wrapped in one of Chuck's puffy winter coats. She's been on the phone this whole time.

"Hey." Orestes looks at the phone in her hand, which lights up with an incoming call. "Where'd you get that?"

"Oh, it's just my agent." She shows him the phone, which reads "A. Parker" and shows a smiling white guy with glasses. "He saw the news, and had a new phone Amazon delivered to your apartment, with his number programmed in."

"In fifteen minutes? With his picture and everything?"

She shrugs and clicks the red button to decline the call. "He's good at his job."

Orestes needs to get a new phone too. His old flip-phone was a casualty of the fight with the Aphid, and he's not sure how he's supposed to find another phone that won't die due to his shocking anxiety.

Then again, looking at the ambulance, which finally drives off, he wonders if he needs to worry about it as much. He's got some new things to discuss with his therapist. Maybe rebalance his meds. He's feeling optimistic for the first time in a long time.

"So you know my Titi, too?" she asks. "I never would have expected they'd be a superhero."

"Wren Fulton." When she frowns, he clarifies. "Child of Mike Gray? The original Shrike? Looks like his kid inherited his powers and mantle after all."

"Oh!" Angel nods. "Mike Gray. Yeah, I've seen his picture in headquarters. Wasn't he the one who went crazy and started murdering ... oh." She trails off, looking uncomfortable.

"Anyway, when I was young, I remember staying with Titi Wren." Angel watches the retreating ambulance. "How do you know so much about this stuff, anyway?"

"Lots of comic books."

Angel snickers. "Ok, nerd. What's the 'Birdie' thing all about? What are they, sixty?"

"The Shrike is a bird that impales its prey on thorns."

"Huh." Angel frowns. "I thought they made that up for that one detective show."

Unsure how to respond, he looks over at her, but she's smiling. They share a laugh.

The reporters have showed up, filming the destroyed building and hunting for anyone who can give them a statement. Chuck is all about the spotlight, and so most of them have taken to interviewing him. It gives Orestes and Angel some cover, like a linesman blocking an oncoming blitz.

"And then I was like, who are you and what are you doing in my space?" he says, "and then pow, Lady Vengeance smacks him one. She's the hero, you know! Saved my life!"

It's heavily embellished, but Orestes has to smile. Angel, on the other hand, pointedly averts her gaze, positioning herself behind him so no one notices her.

Too late. "A-Girl!" shouts one of the reporters, and then the floodgates break open. Journalists, both professional and amateur, come rushing toward them, cameras and phones flashing.

"A-Girl! What happened here tonight?"

"A-Girl! The *Times*—how were you involved? Did you fight the Aphid?"

"Do you have any comment—"

She's the one who knows how to handle this kind of stuff, but she backs away from it, turning her face. It's too much to deal with just now.

He gets that. Casually, Orestes shields her with his body, stepping between her and the press of press. "Hey, it's been a long night, can you just—?"

But that only draws their attention to him, as though they didn't know he was there. Now that they see him, they swarm like sharks. Flashes explode in his face, half-blinding him. Anxiety spikes, and he stammers, unable to think, much less answer questions.

"A-Girl! *Young Ms. American* magazine—who's this man you're with? He's hot!"

"Are you cheating on Blue Steel? A-Girl! What do you say to allegations that you're cheating—"

"A-Girl! Does this mean you're taking a stand against what some are calling the president's anti-Black policies—"

"A-Girl! A-Girl?"

Orestes realizes he's actually floating off the ground. He looks down, only to find Angel's arms wrapped around his midsection, drawing him up. The wind immediately picks up around him, and he knows he should feel afraid, but instead he feels more secure. Safe.

They fly up and onto the top of the building across the street, away from the prying cameras and dazzling flashes. There, she holds onto him a little longer than is strictly necessary, her head pressed into his chest as though she's burrowed into him.

"Um," he says.

She looks up and blinks, startled. "Oh, sorry," she says. "It's just—Aunt V was right, I'm real bad at this flying thing, and I didn't want to drop you. It wouldn't be the first time."

"Oh," he says. "Let's just ... gloss over that second part."

"Deal." She hasn't let go of him, he notices. "Sorry, it's cold up here, and you're, like, really warm."

"Ok," Orestes says. "Isn't that coat—" He trails off, remembering her legs, bare below about mid-thigh. It wasn't like they had more pajama pants she could put on. "You know what? Never mind."

"Thanks." Angel sighs with relief against his chest. "Is this ok? I'm not, like, making you uncomfortable, am I? You'd let me know if I was, like, crushing you or anything."

"No, I mean—yes, it's fine." Orestes smiles. She feels really nice, pressed up against him like that, and she's right, it's freezing up here. "Are *you* ok?"

"I—I'm not sure."

"That's fair."

She took a major hit of fear energy back there. How much did she absorb, before it passed to him? It is absolutely ok for her to not be ok. Neither of them is ok.

They stand there for a while, alone on the roof, looking down over the city. The lights paint Seattle in an amorphous swath of gold and silver, bordered by the flat black sheet of Puget Sound. The wharf is lit up, and the Ferris wheel is still spinning slowly. It's winter in Seattle, where even though it's only 7 p.m. or so, it feels like 11. He rarely sees the city like this—only on planes or the one time his dads took him to the restaurant on top of the Space Needle for his eighteenth birthday this past summer. Let alone has he ever looked at it like this with a girl.

"You know, I've lived here for months, but I've never been up here," he says. "It's pretty sweet."

That sounded stupid the second he said it, but Angel nods in agreement. "Yeah," she says.

"You must see it like this all the time," Orestes says. "You know, flying around."

"Not really," she says. "I mean, like, most of my flying is for photo-shoots and stuff. I don't do a lot of night flying."

"Do you, uh, want to?" Orestes asks.

209

"Hell no," Angel says. "Are you kidding me? I'd smoosh you into something like immediately."

"So you're going to take me flying," he says.

Her eyes widen and her cheeks, which were already red from cold, darken. "I didn't say that."

"Kidding," he says. "It's fine, we can just stand here."

"Ok."

They aren't just standing there, though. She's staring at him, and he at her. Not that he knows what to say, or anything. He's never been good at this.

"Thanks for saving my life," he says. "Tanking those bullets and stuff."

"Oh." Angel smiles. "I guess I did. Ruined your Supergroup shirt though. Was it a collector's item, or anything?"

"Nah," he says, which is absolutely a lie. "So, you know, if I can pay you back or anything—"

"You saved me too, doofus," she says. "Remember? The lightning?"

"Yeah?" It's more of a question than he intends. "I mean, I guess I—"

She leans up and kisses him. His body goes taut, and so does hers, pressing into him.

The kiss lasts only a second, and they pull away from each other. Orestes frowns, and Angel pulls a face and covers her mouth.

"Oh," she says. "Sorry, I—I guess I forgot about the Aphid vomit."

"Yeah," Orestes says.

"I need to brush my teeth," she says. "And take a fucking shower."

"Me too."

They share a smile and another laugh.

Then she extends a hand. "C'mon."

"What?"

"Let's go flying."

Orestes rubs the back of his head. "Aren't you worried you'll smoosh me?"

Angel smiles. "What are you, scared?"

"Terrified." He takes her hand.

They lift off the roof and go flying off into the night.

ABOUT THE AUTHOR

Erik Scott de Bie is a speculative fiction writer whose favored genres include fantasy, sci-fi, horror, and superheroes, and especially pieces that mix all of the above. He is also a known quantity in the gaming industry, being the author and/or editor of a number of major releases for *Dungeons & Dragons*, *Iron Kingdoms*, the Cthulhu Mythos, and others. His most recent novel series is The World of Ruin, a post-apocalyptic fantasy like *Game of Thrones* meets *Fallout*, and he is currently writing in a new gaming tie-in setting for Archvillain Games. He lives in Seattle with his wife and their menagerie of pets. Find him online at https://erikscottdebie.com/.